S0-AEE-706

The Case of The Dangerous Remedy
By Helen Wells

tempo
books

GROSSET & DUNLAP
A FILMWAYS COMPANY
Publishers • New York

Contents

~~~~~~

Acknowledgment

For their valuable help and guidance in the preparation of this book, the author is indebted to:

Miss Martha D. Adam, R.N., Director, Department of Public Health Nursing, National League for Nursing, Inc., New York, N. Y.

Miss Mattie Brass, R.N., Director, Division of Public Health Nursing, Iowa State Department of Health, Des Moines, Iowa.

Mr. Wallace F. Janssen, Director, Division of Public Information, Department of Health, Education and Welfare, Food and Drug Administration, Washington, D. C.

CHAPTER I

New Job, New Friends

"WELL, NOW YOU'RE ON YOUR OWN, CHERRY AMES," said the nurse supervisor. "Now you'll be the one and only nurse responsible for good public health nursing service in this entire county. Just you, Cherry."

"I'm scared and delighted all at once," Cherry said. "All those families! We visited only a sampling of them. All those towns and villages!"

Cherry and Miss Hudson had just returned from their last visit together to the twenty-five square miles of Cherry's county in southeastern Iowa. It was a lovely countryside of thriving farms, where some ten thousand persons lived and worked, and where their children attended rural schools.

"Scared or not," Cherry said, "I feel I'm off to a good start, Miss Hudson. I learned a lot driving around with you, nursing under your supervision during this training period."

"I think you'll do fine," her supervisor encouraged her. "I'll visit you regularly, and you'll come to monthly meetings with my fourteen other county nurses. Between times, if you need any advice or extra help, you can always phone or write me at the regional office upstate. Of course all the specialized facilities of the State Health Department are open to your patients on your request." Miss Hudson smiled at her reassuringly. "And Dr. Miller, as health officer and your medical adviser, will confer with you frequently here in your office."

Cherry had been assigned this rather bare office on the second floor of the county courthouse in the small, quiet town of Sauk. Sunlight sifting through the trees outside shone on file cabinets and tables' stacked with county health records and pamphlets about community health.

"I'm glad," Cherry admitted, "that Dr. Hal Miller is young and as new on his county job as I am on mine. Makes it easier to work comfortably together."

The supervisor smiled. "Well, you have to be young and strong to go out in all kinds of weather to nurse patients deep in the country. And I shouldn't say just 'patients.' Remember that well people, who can be prevented from getting sick, are just as big a part of your job, Cherry. Remember to *teach* good health care, and plan it in terms of whole communities."

"I'll remember," Cherry said.

She felt rather breathless at the scope of her "one-man" job. Nursing new babies, children's diseases, old people, and persons hurt in farm accidents, nursing patients of the eight physicians scattered through-out the county, under the physicians' direction—that was only part of it. She would also teach health at P.T.A. meetings; keep watch for any threatened epidemic; and, if necessary, set up emergency clinics under the direction of the county health officer. She'd have TB control work to do, too. And she'd act as the one and only school nurse at the twenty-odd rural schools in her county. The nearest hospital was twenty-five miles away. It was a tall order for one nurse.

"I'm lucky," she thought, "to be working with a county doctor as nice as Hal Miller."

Miss Hudson picked up her handbag and a sheaf of reports. She smothered a yawn. "Thank goodness it's Saturday, and the beginning of Labor Day week end."

Cherry walked downstairs with her supervisor. "You still have a long drive home, haven't you, Miss Hudson? Before you start out, would you like to come over to my Aunt Cora's house and have some iced tea?"

Aunt Cora, Cherry knew, could be counted on for hospitality at the drop of a hat. Hadn't she taken Cherry herself in to stay at her comfortable house here in Sauk? Aunt Cora was one big reason Cherry had applied for this position as rural nurse.

"Thanks, Cherry, but I promised my own family to be home for supper." Miss Hudson opened her car door and held out her hand to Cherry. "Good luck."

Just then another car pulled up alongside the

supervisor's. A tall, lean, young man in a rumpled suit jumped out and came over to the two nurses. A thermometer in its case stuck out of his breast pocket, and a late garden rose was in his lapel.

"Are you leaving now, Miss Hudson?" Dr. Hal Miller asked. "I tried to get here sooner, but I had to stay with the Ellis youngster until his hemorraghing stopped. Hello, Miss Cherry."

Cherry smiled at the young physician, and Miss Hudson said to him, "It's nice of you to see me off. We'll be meeting again soon in some of the state or university hospitals. Now if I don't get started, I'll *never* leave this lovely little old town."

The supervisor slid into her car, waved, and drove off. Dr. Miller and Cherry stood for a minute in the shade of the courthouse trees. He mopped his forehead with his handkerchief.

"Had a busy afternoon, Doctor?" Cherry asked, with a hint of a smile.

He grinned back at her. "You look a little warm and dusty yourself. Say, would you mind coming back upstairs for a quick conference? I know it's late, I know we aren't supposed to work as a regular thing on Saturdays, but the work does pile up."

"Of course I don't mind," Cherry said. Sick people, and prevention of sickness, could not wait. Besides, Cherry knew, Dr. Miller had his hands full as both the county health officer and private practitioner. He shared an office with, and assisted, Dr. Aloysius Clark, who was growing too old to drive long distances in the country. The young doctor drove out to treat these rural patients.

Some of Cherry's patients, unable to pay, would be treated without charge by Dr. Miller as county health officer. Other patients, able to pay, would be treated privately by any of the county doctors, who would call Cherry in to do the necessary nursing. Many times her patients would be persons she herself discovered to be in need of health care and referred to a doctor.

Cherry and Dr. Hal talked over the day's cases and made plans for next week's visits. The big bare room grew shadowy. The young doctor closed the last case folder while Cherry finished writing down his nursing instructions.

"There! That's all we can do for today," he said. "There's nothing that can't safely wait over the week end. Gosh, I'm starving!"

Cherry looked over her shoulder. "It's so late, even my clerk has gone home."

Dr. Hal got up and stretched his long arms and legs. "Miss Cherry, did you feel as overheated all day as I did? Calendar says September third, but I thought I'd melt."

"The heat's good, makes the corn ripen," Cherry quoted her farmer friends. "Yes, Doctor, the sun felt so warm today I wanted to go swimming."

"Well, why don't we?" Dr. Miller suggested. "Swimming weather isn't going to last much longer. Why don't we round up some people, and have a picnic and swim at Riverside Park?"

Cherry was interested. "Tomorrow? Or Monday? That's Labor Day." She had a moment's hesitation about whether it would be all right for her to see Dr.

Hal socially. They had not yet done so, unless she counted accidentally meeting him at the town's one drugstore or garage or seeing him at church. Both of them had been crowded for time, she with in-job training, and he in learning his duties as part-time health officer. But now——? Well, Cherry decided, formal medical etiquette need not apply in a little backwoods town like Sauk, where there was only a handful of people to be friends with one another.

Dr. Hal must have been thinking much the same thing, for he said:

"You know, Miss Cherry—darn it, let's drop the formalities when we're not working. Can't I call you Cherry, and you call me Hal?"

Cherry smiled and nodded. "Yes, Doctor," she said to tease him. He was only a few years older than she was, so it felt perfectly natural to be friends.

"Well, you know, Cherry," he said, perching on a desk, "it's a funny thing how I haven't gotten around to seeing you except on the job. I've wanted to. In fact, since I came to Sauk, I haven't spent time with anyone except medical personnel and patients. Maybe that's what comes of working *and* living at Dr. Clark's house. Hmmm? Why, now that we spoke of having a swimming party, I realize I don't know any people to invite except one next-door neighbor."

"Well, I only know my next-door neighbors and the Drew girls," Cherry said. "I'm still new here, too. Never mind. My Aunt Cora knows everybody for miles around here. She'll gather up some acquaintances for us."

"Your Aunt Cora sounds grand."

"She is. And if I don't go home to supper soon, she may send Sheriff Steeley after me."

Dr. Hal decided to leave his car parked where it was, and walk home. The tree-filled main street was only eight blocks long and part of a federal highway. They met no one else out walking at this hour; people were indoors having their suppers. Only the birds were in sight, swooping and twittering as the sun dropped. Cherry felt relaxed, and listened to the young man walking beside her.

Hal told Cherry he came from a small town like this one, but in another part of Iowa. He had taken his medical training at the fine schools here in his home state. Then he had served as intern and, later, as staff physician at a large hospital in St. Louis, Missouri.

"I didn't feel at home working in a big institution," he said. "I didn't like the rigid routine. I missed my own country kind of people. Besides, I felt cooped up in the city. So I looked for an opening in a rural area, and the United States Public Health Service gave me a scholarship and trained me as a health officer. Then a former professor of mine wrote that his old friend, Dr. Clark, was looking for a husky young assistant. So here I am." He smiled down a little shyly at Cherry. "What about you? You did tell me a few things about your training, the different kinds of nursing you've done, but I'd like to hear more."

It embarrassed Cherry to talk about herself. As they turned the next corner, she could see Aunt Cora's straight figure standing on the front porch, farther up the street. Cherry mumbled, "My aunt must think I'm lost, strayed, or stolen," and walked faster.

Dr. Hal looked amused and quickened his long, easy stride. "Well, you'll have to tell me some other time. Especially about why you wanted to have a try at rural nursing."

"That's easy. I was born and brought up across the Mississippi River east from here, in Illinois, in a town in the heart of the corn belt. I've always known and respected the people who grow the nation's food, and I've always had a hankering to—to nurse out in the country."

"Did anyone ever tell you you're awfully pretty?" Dr. Hal said. She was tall and slim and full of life, with brilliant dark eyes and dark curls. "Did those cherry-red cheeks win you your name?"

"Thank you for the kind remarks," Cherry said. "No, I'm named for my grandmother. My coloring turned out to be sort of—uh—an appropriate accident."

Dr. Hal burst out laughing at that. They had reached Aunt Cora's house. Cherry noticed in surprise that her aunt wore her next-to-best flowered silk dress, and two cars were parked in front of the house. One was her aunt's sleek new car, the other was a rusty black sedan, so old, big, and cumbersome that it resembled a boat or a hearse. What was going on?

Aunt Cora came down the steps, shaking her head but smiling.

"Where in the world have you been, child? You're Dr. Hal Miller, aren't you? I've wanted to meet you ever since Aloysius told me about you. I'm sorry to snatch Cherry away, but an old friend of mine has just come home after being away all summer, and we're celebrating by going out for supper. I certainly hope you'll come by another time, and often—"

"Thank you, Mrs. Ames. You may be seeing me sooner than you count on. Cherry, will you ask your aunt about the picnic?"

"What picnic?" Aunt Cora wanted to know.

"Why," Cherry said, "the picnic and swimming party that we hope you're going to arrange for us. For tomorrow or Labor Day."

Aunt Cora looked baffled, but recovered immediately. "Do you want fried chicken to take along, or wieners and potatoes to roast over a bonfire? And for how many of you?"

"Ah—we don't know enough people yet to ask," Dr. Hal admitted.

"I'll get to work on it by telephone," Aunt Cora promised. "I know ever so many young people who'd like to know you. Well! I'm glad you both are finally taking a little time off from work to socialize! How many young people do you want me to invite? Ten? Twenty?"

"Mrs. Ames, you're wonderful," said the young man. "If I can help, let me know—and many, many thanks. I'll be in touch to ask whether it'll be tomorrow or Monday."

He looked so eager, Cherry could see he hoped it would be tomorrow. He continued down the quiet street, whistling.

"You *are* wonderful," Cherry said to Aunt Cora, and hugged her. "You won't mind being hostess, will you?"

"*You'll* be the hostess—no, no, I'm not going along. You young people will have more fun by yourselves. Don't worry about getting acquainted. In ten minutes you'll all be old friends."

"I'm anything but worried!" Cherry said. "I'm just delighted at the prospect of a picnic with new friends."

"And with young Dr. Miller?" Her aunt gave her a shrewd look, which turned into a smile. "I saw you and that nice young doctor ambling down the street together at a snail's pace."

"Have I detained you? I'm sorry, Aunt Cora. We were working at the office, honestly."

"Oh, a few minutes' delay doesn't matter, honey. Except that my friend Phoebe is waiting for us. She's real interested in meeting my niece. She hasn't seen you since you were three and fell in the duckpond."

"I hope I've improved since then," Cherry said, and followed her aunt into the house.

~~~~~~

CHAPTER II

Guest at Aunt Cora's

CHERRY WAS VERY FOND OF AUNT CORA—REALLY
an older cousin by marriage—whom she had seen
and known only in snatches all her life. Aunt Cora
and her husband, Jim Ames, had always traveled a
great deal, and sometimes had stopped off in Cherry's home town on their way to Bombay or Paris or
Copenhagen. Now that Aunt Cora was a widow and
"not as young as she used to be," she stayed at home,
enjoying her comfortable house and garden and her
books and her many community activities. She had
written to the Ameses that she would enjoy having
some young company in the house.

Cherry's twin brother, Charlie, was too busy and
fascinated with his aviation engineering job in In-
dianapolis to be able to visit her. But Aunt Cora's in-
vitation had found Cherry between jobs and thinking
about what sort of nursing job she would like to try
next. She had read in a professional bulletin last
summer that R.N.'s were needed as rural nurses,

and on inquiring, had learned there were job openings in Iowa, in Sauk County, in fact.

From there on, it had been a matter of taking and passing the written examinations given by Iowa's Merit System, similar to Civil Service, and undergoing field training. It helped that Cherry earlier had trained and worked as a visiting nurse in New York City. It helped further that the Visiting Nurse Service had allowed Cherry time to go to college part time and take the advanced courses required in public health nursing.

Now she was ready for a highly independent sort of job, and very much at home in Aunt Cora's roomy, flower-filled house. Aunt Cora's choicest African violets grew in white pots in the living room, and Mrs. Phoebe Grisbee was fussing over them.

"I declare, Cora, why don't you tamp down a little tobacco on the soil? Oh, here's your niece! My, Cherry, you certainly have changed since you fell in with the ducks!"

"I should hope so," Aunt Cora said amiably, and Cherry took Mrs. Grisbee's outstretched hand.

Her aunt's friend was a plump, plainly dressed woman with spectacles and a big smile on her round face. She had never been farther away from home than St. Louis, and still held to many of the ideas and ways of living she had learned as a girl growing up on a farm near here.

Cherry said, "I'm glad to see you, Mrs. Grisbee," and thought that Phoebe Grisbee, whether as dowdy as her old car or not, must be an awfully nice person for Aunt Cora to be lifelong friends with her.

"Mr. Grisbee," Mrs. Grisbee explained to Cherry, "is at home all by himself, poor soul, though I did invite him. You know how Mr. Grisbee is about hen parties, Cora, and restaurant food."

"Yes, I know Henry's not a ladies' man," said Aunt Cora. "We three ladies," she said, turning to Cherry, "are about to have supper at Sauk's one and only restaurant."

"At least I left a nice supper for him," said Phoebe Grisbee, worrying about her husband, "and a pot of his favorite herb tea keeping hot on the stove. Cherry, you're a nurse, you'd know about the healthful value of herbs?"

"Mmm—well, perhaps certain herbs," Cherry said. She wondered how much reliance Mrs. Grisbee put in farm lore and how much in tested scientific discoveries. "I don't mean to sound official, but herbs haven't much value, except a few as a mild tonic, Mrs. Grisbee. Modern medical science provides much better medications."

"Phoebe knows that perfectly well," Aunt Cora said. "If she sets any store by herbs, it's because she takes pleasure growing them in her garden."

Mrs. Grisbee nodded mildly. "Speaking of medicines, Miss Nurse," she said, "we may be in the backwoods, but we can buy the best just the same. Our local drugstore and the door-to-door salesmen take good care of us."

"What door-to-door salesmen?" Cherry asked.

"Oh, the Watkins Company man comes through these parts about six times a year," Mrs. Grisbee said. "He's due pretty soon again. You watch, out there on the country roads, and you'll see a man driving a smart-looking delivery truck and going from farm to farm selling his wares. He sells a certain amount in towns, too, but mostly it's to the farmers."

Aunt Cora explained to Cherry that some farm people were isolated and did not have much time to travel into the nearest town to shop; besides, a town like Sauk offered only limited supplies. Therefore, door-to-door salesmen and local peddlers brought the needed merchandise to the farmers.

"What do they sell?" Cherry asked. She remembered seeing door-to-door salesmen occasionally in and around her home town, but Hilton was not as rural as here. "You mentioned that they sell medicines—I guess you mean patent medicines?"

"That's right, patent medicine," Phoebe Grisbee said. "Oh, liniment and cough syrup and vitamins and laxative herb tablets, and lots of other home remedies. And livestock remedies, and insect spray, and even toothpaste and vanilla and— Why, I buy all my needles and thread from Mr. Carlson; he has the best. And I count on Old Snell, whenever he turns up, for certain of my herbs and berries—he gathers 'em in the woods."

"That's a real convenience," said Cherry.

"Well, you'll soon be educated in country ways," said Aunt Cora. "Now, honey, if you're planning to change out of that uniform—"

"I'll be quick," Cherry promised.

Cherry freshened up in a hurry, brushed her dark curls until they shone, and put on a crisp red-and-white gingham dress.

As they strolled the few blocks to downtown, the three women stopped to chat with friends along the way. Their neighbors were just coming out on their porches in the early evening. "Anybody for a picnic and swimming party, tomorrow or Monday?" Aunt Cora asked several young people. The Drew sisters accepted right away, and asked whether the picnic could be Sunday. They, and the Anderson young people, had made plans to visit relatives on Labor Day. Passing Dr. Clark's white frame house on Main Street, Cherry decided to ask the housekeeper to tell Dr. Miller: "Picnic *tomorrow.*"

On the rest of their walk down Main Street they met a crowd. Farmers with their entire families had driven in for Saturday night in town. The few stores were open and brightly lighted, jammed to the doors with shoppers. Boys and girls crowded into the one movie theater and stood three deep around the drugstore soda fountain. Cherry overheard someone say there was a dance starting for the young folks one block over, at the school.

Smith's Restaurant was the last building in the row of stores and upstairs offices. Beyond, in shadow now, were the bank, the post office, the public library, and the courthouse with lights burning in the sheriff's office. Cherry looked toward the courthouse for the windows of her office, through the dark trees, until her aunt nudged her. They went into the restaurant.

Smith's had a busy lunchroom counter in front, and in back, a dining room with tables and a few booths. "The dining room is nearly always empty,"

Mrs. Grisbee said. "It's a dandy place to gossip."

Mostly they talked about plans for tomorrow's picnic, over platters of steak sandwiches and home-grown tomatoes, and about Mrs. Grisbee's visit this summer with her sister in Missouri, just south across the Des Moines River and the state line. They discussed Cherry's new job, and her new little car, waiting for her in Michaels' Garage. Half of the car was a present from her dad, the other half she'd paid for herself out of savings. The county, which employed her, would pay her mileage allowance for operating the car on her calls to patients. The car was bright blue, small, inexpensive to run, and easy to park. Cherry was immensely pleased with it. On their walk home she peeked in the garage to see it. Mrs. Grisbee said her car could stay parked overnight where it was. Cherry and Aunt Cora left Mrs. Grisbee at her house—Cherry could smell the spicy herbs from her herb garden, somewhere in the dark. Then Cherry and Aunt Cora went home. Aunt Cora systematically telephoned for miles around about the picnic, with Cherry sitting beside her. Not many young persons were at home on a warm, starry Saturday night. Those who were at home accepted with glee.

"Well," said Aunt Cora, half an hour later, "I'll try telephoning again bright and early tomorrow morning. I think plenty will be glad to go."

Aunt Cora went to the open door, stepped out on the porch, and looked up at the night sky. Stars were out in profusion, and hanging over the treetops was a big, yellow, harvest moon.

"You'll have a fine day tomorrow," she said to Cherry beside her.

"I think we'll have a fine day in more ways than the weather, Aunt Cora."

"Deader than a doornail" was how Aunt Cora described her home town. Considering that Sauk was a very small farming town in the southeast corner of Iowa, close to where the Des Moines River flows down into the Mississippi, Aunt Cora was right. Except on this fine Sunday morning! Right after church, four cars full of young persons stirred up a great deal of laughter and excitement, assembling in front of Cora Ames's house. They were loaded down with picnic baskets, bathing suits, cameras, a guitar that belonged to plump Joe Mercer— and they raised a cheerful hullabaloo in getting acquainted with Cherry and Dr. Hal. Neighbors on their way home from church stopped, stared, and smiled.

The four cars sped off and the carefree picnickers burst into song. Cherry was squeezed in the second car—Dr. Hal's car—with the Van Tine brothers and the Drew girls. In two minutes flat they had left Sauk, and were rolling along on the open highway. Riverside Park was some ten miles away, "kerplunk in the middle of our territory," Dr. Hal said. The sun beat down, the fields were still green with the crops of late summer. Dick Van Tine said their father was already getting ready to plant a stand of winter wheat.

The road followed along the broad Des Moines

River, as it came flowing down from still farther west and north. Road and river turned together, and their four cars passed an overgrown farm, with a rickety farmhouse standing far back from the highway. Cherry could see the blue river glinting behind the farmhouse. Then they drove past a woods, and turned into the dirt roadway of Riverside Park.

Once this site had been a forest where Indians camped and fished. It still was half wild, except for a few picnic tables, a log house with lockers for bathers, and an outdoor telephone booth. Cherry went with Dr. Hal while he hunted up a lean youth who was renting rowboats at the river's edge.

"Hello, Ezra," the young doctor said. "Do you know our new county nurse?" He introduced Cherry. "Ezra, Dr. Clark is out of town for the holiday week end, and anyway I'm always on county call. I've instructed his housekeeper, and also the telephone operators, in case there's an emergency, to phone me here at the park. I'm the only doctor available around here this week end. You'll be sure to let me know if a call comes in?"

"Sure thing, Dr. Miller."

The youth turned back to his rowboats. Dr. Hal and Cherry rejoined their new friends.

Swimming came first on the program. The water felt warm with the sun on it. On the opposite shore, the neighboring state of Missouri was so near at one point, where the river narrowed, that three of the young men swam across and back. "We've just been to Missouri," they announced. "Sorry we didn't think to send you post cards."

After drying off in the sun and getting dressed again, they all had lunch. It tasted especially good outdoors. Then the picnickers split up to do a variety of things. Cherry, Dr. Hal, and roly-poly Joe Mercer wanted to go exploring.

Starting off by themselves, they walked along the river's edge. Presently Joe Mercer announced, "Excuse me, but I'm going back to eat that last piece of apple pie before the squirrels get it." He jogged off, leaving Cherry and Dr. Hal laughing.

"Well, I don't mind being a twosome," Dr. Hal said gallantly to Cherry.

They strolled along the shore, sometimes ducking under low branches, pausing to admire fern and the first red berries of autumn. They had not gone far when something in deep shadow caught Cherry's attention.

"What's that?" she said. "Let's go see."

She pushed through underbrush several paces inland. Dr. Hal, following her, pointed out a few flat, worn rocks that suggested an old trail. "But I don't see anything, Cherry."

"If you'll help me pull this low branch aside—"

They swung the half-concealing branch to one side, and before them yawned the low, rocky opening of a cave. Its interior was inky black.

"I didn't know there was a cave here, so close to the river," Dr. Hal said. "And I've been to this park a few times."

"It certainly is dark in there," said Cherry. She already had one foot inside the cave. "Come on! I thought you wanted to explore."

"Careful," Dr. Hal said. He struck a match, and they entered the cave together. Dr. Hal had to stoop to get in.

The cave was low-ceilinged, small, and craggy. Cautiously, step by step, they walked deeper into the cave. The air was chill and damp. Dr. Hal struck more matches, and the flame threw grotesque shadows. When Cherry spoke, her voice sent back whispery echoes.

"We'd better not go too far in. I can't see any end to this." Sometimes a cave led into an interior cave, and still another, like a catacomb of rooms. It might be unsafe to go farther.

"I think I see something," Dr. Hal muttered. "Just ahead—if my matches hold out—"

Dr. Hal sprinted forward. Cherry followed him. They were brought to a halt by a wooden barrier.

"It's nothing but an old barn door," Dr. Hal said disgustedly. He examined it, shook it, but it held firm. "Someone wedged it in here pretty tight, I guess," he said. "Or this old barn door has been left in here for so long that it's half sunk into the cave walls by now."

"Why would anyone drag an old barn door in here?" Cherry wanted to know.

"Oh, kids do things like that when they're playing. Didn't you ever play cops and robbers, or hide-and-seek, in places like this? I used to. Well, this is the far end of the cave, I guess."

"Or is it?" Cherry asked. "Could that old barn door be the door *to* something?"

Dr. Hal knocked on the rotting wood. "It doesn't

sound as if there's anything on the other side," he said. "Only the back wall of the cave, at a guess." His match went out, his last one.

Someone was calling them. The call came from near the mouth of the cave, a man's voice shouting:

"Doc-tor! Doc-tor!"

Cherry and Dr. Hal groped their way as fast as they could toward the patch of daylight at the cave's opening. There stood Joe Mercer, puffing and puzzled.

"Oh, so that's where you disappeared to!" Joe Mercer said. "I've been hollering all around here. Ezra has a telephone message for you, Doctor. Emergency."

"Thanks." Dr. Hal started off at a run. Cherry hurried after him, hoping that the holiday emergency was not more than one doctor and one nurse could handle.

CHAPTER III

Jane's Story

ONCE DR. HAL HAD EZRA'S MESSAGE, HE AND CHERRY were obliged to say good-by to their guests. "Come back if you can," their friends called, as Cherry and Hal drove out of Riverside Park. On the way back to town Dr. Hal told Cherry what the message was.

Half an hour before, a young woman, a stranger, had gotten off the train at Sauk. While carrying her suitcase and looking around for a telephone or a taxi, she had stumbled over a rut in the road. She had fallen and broken her ankle. A passer-by and the druggist had applied a temporary splint and carried her to Dr. Clark's house. Dr. Clark's housekeeper had telephoned Dr. Hal.

Dr. Hal planned to examine the patient and set the ankle in Dr. Clark's well-equipped medical office, he told Cherry. "You'll assist me," he said. "Mrs. King—that's the housekeeper—is helpful, but she's not a nurse."

As soon as they arrived at Dr. Clark's house, they

quickly scrubbed, donned clean white cotton coats, and went into the examining room. A brown-haired young woman was resting on a couch. Mrs. King, who was with the patient, had covered her with a light blanket and had already given her a cup of hot tea. The housekeeper looked relieved as the doctor and nurse came in.

"Dr. Miller, Nurse, this is Miss Jane Fraser. She's just come here from New York to—to—"

"—to fall down and break my ankle," the young woman said, and grinned in spite of her evident pain. She was about Cherry's age, very pleasant looking, trimly dressed in a cotton suit which had smears of dust and gasoline on it. "What a way to arrive!"

"Never mind, we'll soon fix you up," Dr. Hal said. He looked at the ankle, which was swelling. "You're alone, Miss Fraser? Haven't you anyone here to take care of you?"

"Well, I— Someone was supposed to meet me with a car, but he didn't show up, I don't know why—" The young woman swallowed hard. "I'm to stay at Mrs. Barker's house, out in the country. She's the only person I know here. But she's an old lady and can't come to get me, and her son didn't meet my train. Sorry to be thrown on your mercy."

"That's what we're here for." The tall young doctor smiled at her. "This is Cherry Ames, our county nurse. Mrs. King, do you know our nurse?"

Cherry smiled at the housekeeper and at the young woman. It was hard enough for anyone to sustain an injury, but to be alone and helpless in a strange place must be hard indeed.

"You mustn't worry, Miss Fraser," said Cherry. "We'll see that you reach Mrs. Barker's, won't we, Dr. Miller?" He nodded. "The doctor and I will come and check on how your ankle progresses."

"That's wonderful," Jane Fraser said. She was so grateful that tears came to her eyes. "Mrs. King has already been so kind to me, you're all so kind to a stranger. I—I can't pay much, hardly anything for your—"

Dr. Hal told her a reasonable fee could be arranged. The housekeeper, after inquiring whether she would be needed further, left the room. Dr. Hal set to work.

This was the first time Cherry had worked with Dr. Hal Miller on a fracture case. She was impressed with the skill and gentleness of his big hands. First, with her aid, he took an X ray of the ankle, using Dr. Clark's X-ray machine, then developed it. As Dr. Hal lightly probed the broken bones of the ankle with his finger tips, the pain made Jane hold tight to Cherry's hand. Then Dr. Hal injected a local anesthetic. Very carefully, scowling with concentration, he set the ankle, bringing the bones into proper alignment with one another. Then, with Cherry assisting, Dr. Miller put a plaster cast on the ankle, to hold the bones firmly in place. Finally he took another X ray to check that everything was in good order.

"All finished. You're a good patient," he said to Jane Fraser. "Not a murmur out of you. And you, Miss Ames, are a good nurse."

"We both thank you, don't we?" Cherry said.

Jane Fraser smiled weakly. "I feel as if I'm among friends."

"You are," Dr. Hal said. "That ankle will take time to heal, but you'll be able to get around within a few days. This is the lightest-weight cast, and we'll lend you a pair of crutches. That's not so bad, is it?"

"That's fine, because I have an awful lot of urgent things to do around here," Jane Fraser said. "And such a short time to do them all." She looked anxious.

"Don't overdo," Dr. Hal cautioned her. "And don't put your weight on the cast. Rest half an hour now. Then we'll drive you to Mrs. Barker's."

Cherry tried to telephone Mrs. Barker, but the party line was busy continuously on a holiday, and Cherry could not reach her.

It was late afternoon by the time the three of them were on the highway in Dr. Hal's car. They had propped Jane Fraser across the back seat as comfortably as they could manage, with her foot elevated on a pillow. Cherry turned around to talk with her. Jane told them that she was a nutritionist, that all the family she had was her mother, and that she was engaged to be married.

"We're going to get married even if Bill never gets completely well!" Jane said. "He *may* be cured someday, if I can just swing things here in Iowa." She did not say what was the matter with her fiancé.

"You sound worried," Cherry said sympathetically.

Jane forced a lighter tone. "I guess if I weren't so worried about what I hope to do here, and so excited and overtired, I wouldn't have stumbled and awarded myself a fractured ankle. A great help I am, *not*."

Dr. Hal, driving, looked concerned but kept silent. Cherry said encouragingly to Jane, "Could be worse. We'll have you walking around on crutches by tomorrow."

They stopped at a crossroads store to inquire where Mrs. Barker's place was, since neither Dr. Hal nor Cherry knew. Jane Fraser did not know, either. She said she had been in Iowa once when she was about four years old, with her mother, and had met Mrs. Barker and her son then, but she could not remember either the place or the people. She knew Mrs. Barker, an old acquaintance of her mother's, only through letters.

The Barker place was a mile beyond Riverside Park. It was a scrap of land in these vast plains, only about three acres, with a flimsy cottage, one cow, a shed, a few chickens, and a vegetable patch. Mrs. Barker must be poor, Cherry thought. But the place was as clean and tidy as the old lady who came bustling out to greet them.

"Jane! Is that you, Jane? Land's sakes, where have you been?" Mrs. Barker looked at the three young people in bewilderment. "Young man, aren't you the new doctor?"

"Yes, ma'am," he said, and Cherry thought she'd be inclined, too, to say a respectful "yes, ma'am" to this vigorous little woman of sixty.

"Which one of you girls is Jane?" Mrs. Barker asked. "Why in the world are you so late? And where's Floyd? Didn't he meet you?"

Dr. Miller introduced Jane and Cherry, and explained gently what had happened. The old lady looked ready to cry, but she said:

"Well, what's done is done. I'm mighty sorry about your accident, Jane. I'll take good care of you. That shiftless son of mine! If he had met you, like he promised me, maybe you wouldn't have taken that tumble. I can't count on Floyd for a single, blessed thing," she said sadly, half to herself. "Well! Come on, children, let's get this girl into the house."

Jane managed slowly with the crutches and help from Dr. Hal. Cherry went ahead with Mrs. Barker into the cottage. The living room was small and crowded with an assortment of worn-out furniture. A parrot greeted Cherry with "Good-by! Good-by!"

"He'll say hello to you when you leave," Mrs. Barker said. "His name is Mike. That bird is an embarrassment to me, the way he repeats our conversations sometimes, but he's company."

The old lady sounded lonely. Cherry inquired whether anyone else besides her son Floyd lived here. No one else, Mrs. Barker said. She led the way into the small spare bedroom which was to be Jane's. Cherry helped Mrs. Barker turn down the bedcovers, since Jane would need to rest.

Hal helped Jane slowly into the spare room, and she sank down on the bed. Dr. Hal gave a few simple instructions to Mrs. Barker for Jane's care, and told the patient:

"Now don't worry about a thing. Just rest. Miss Cherry and I will come back tomorrow."

Cherry said a few encouraging words to Jane Fraser, and said good-by to Mrs. Barker. Then she

and Dr. Hal left, with the parrot calling after them:
"Hello! Hello!"

The next day Dr. Hal held a conference with
Cherry as they drove up to the Barkers' cottage on
Labor Day afternoon.

"The main problem, I think," Dr. Hal said, "is
to keep Jane in good general health, so she'll have
the vitality needed for the ankle to heal. As it is, that
girl seems tired to the point of exhaustion."

"And worried half to death," Cherry said. "That's
a large part of what's draining her energies, isn't it?"

"Her health problem may be mostly a problem of
morale," Dr. Hal agreed. "Let's see whether we can
get Jane to talk about what's worrying her. She might
find it a relief to unburden herself. We'll have time
to visit with her today, since it's a holiday. Hey, look
at that museum piece in the Barkers' yard!"

Dr. Hal braked to a stop and they both stared. Next
to the well, someone had parked a rusty old jalopy.
It looked ready to fall to pieces, but apparently it
worked, for a pair of man's rubber boots and a tin
bucket of grapes were on the front seat.

"Might be Floyd's," Cherry said.

"Maybe," Dr. Hal said, "Floyd didn't meet Jane
because that contraption never made it as far as the
railroad station."

That, in fact, was Floyd's excuse. Mrs. Barker
told them so when she came out and led them into
the house. She took the grapes in with her.

"I wish my son would've stayed home a few minutes to meet you folks," Mrs. Barker apologized.

"But Floyd always has some business of his own to attend to. I never know where he's off to."

They found Jane sitting beside a sunny open window in the spare bedroom. She was writing a letter when they came in, but eagerly put it aside.

"You look much better today," Dr. Hal said. He examined Jane's leg around the cast, to make sure that circulation was normal, and asked Jane a few questions. Cherry made notes for him, for Jane Fraser's record.

"This girl isn't sick," Cherry said cheerfully. "Just incapacitated temporarily."

"But I can't afford to be incapacitated!" Jane exclaimed. "Not when I need to make every single day here count!"

"You're in Iowa on a very special errand, aren't you?" Cherry said.

"Yes. But now, with this ankle—" Jane shook her head. "To come all this distance for nothing— Bill and I may never get married now."

"Maybe we can help you with your special errand," Dr. Hal suggested.

"Yes, maybe we can," Cherry said, and sat down in the sun beside Jane to listen.

The girl sighed, then told them her story. When she and Bill Dowd became engaged, they had to find ways to provide a home for themselves and Jane's mother. Jane's salary as a nutritionist was small, and so were Bill's earnings as a salesman. So he took a risky job which paid well. Bill had done deep-sea diving for sport and—thinking himself strong and

well—went to work diving to mine underwater baux-
ite. He did heavy labor for long hours in the cold
water, off the coast of Brazil, and worked several
long, rainy, sea voyages on a freighter between the
United States and Brazil. As a result, Bill contracted
tuberculosis. For over two years, he had been in hospitals; the money he earned had gone to pay for his
hospital bills.

"I feel responsible for the tuberculosis," Jane said.
"He won't be able to work for a very long time to
come. If ever." She added, "Bill has no family, no
one but me to look out for him."

From the way she spoke, Cherry could see that
Jane and Bill were very much in love, still wanted to
marry—and they had already had a long wait.

Jane sighed. "My mother feels bad, too, about
our situation. She wants to help Bill and me all she
can—by keeping house while I work, and doing
whatever nursing Bill may need."

Cherry and Dr. Hal looked at Jane with sympathy.
There was not much to say in the face of such hard-
ship. Dr. Hal asked what medical care Bill had had.

The past two years, Jane said, he had been at a
TB sanitarium in upstate New York. Although Bill
was better now, and no longer needed much medical care, he was a long way from full recovery. In
fact, the doctors recently told him and Jane that his
recovery depended on living quietly in the country,
and of course doing no heavy work.

"That news was a blow," Jane said. "We'd thought
that after two years' rest and care, he'd be much bet-

ter than he is. We didn't know what to do next."

Neither Bill nor Jane could afford to keep him on at the sanitarium. The only alternative was for him to go to a free, public, country hospital—where he was at present. This meant that he and Jane would be separated indefinitely. Before they could ever marry and be together, they had to get a home in the country—but there was no money.

"Then"—Jane's face lighted up —"I received a letter from an attorney's office, out of the blue. A great-uncle of mine—I scarcely can remember him —my mother's uncle—died and left me a small farm around here. About a mile from here."

"Why, that's wonderful!" Cherry exclaimed.

Jane smiled uncertainly. "We rejoiced, maybe too soon. That old farm *could* be the answer to our problem. But there's an *if*. Wait—it's not what you think. Here's what I planned."

Jane had figured she could, as a nutritionist, find a job in one of the many mills, canneries, or dairies in this farm area. Or she could apply in the thriving small towns around here at a large motel restaurant, school, or hospital. Jane was willing to buy an inexpensive used car and drive many miles to her job, if necessary, while her mother would keep house. Her husband-to-be would do whatever outdoor activity on the farm that his doctors would advise, perhaps none. Jane and her family did not plan to work the old farm, except for a vegetable patch.

"Living in the country can be inexpensive," Jane said. "The main thing is a house! Once we have a house, the three of us could manage on my salary.

Eventually Bill can find some gainful occupation he can do at home, once he grows stronger."

"You're a brave girl," said Dr. Hal. "You said there's an *if*—?"

Jane pushed back her soft brown hair. "Yes, another letter came. From Mrs. Barker, this time."

She paused to explain that the Barkers were distant cousins of the deceased great-uncle. They had been his neighbors until the old man had abandoned his farm and moved to California several years ago.

"I vaguely remember his farm," Jane said. "My mother brought me West to see him once when I was very small. We were his nearest kin. Mother says it was during that visit that she and Emma Barker met and became friends, and they've exchanged Christmas cards and an occasional letter ever since. When I inherited the old place, Mother wrote Mrs. Barker the news. Well," Jane said slowly, "Mrs. Barker wrote back—"

Mrs. Barker invited Jane to stay with her, while she decided what to do about the old farm. Mrs. Barker said in her letter that ever since the great-uncle had abandoned the farm, it had become overgrown with weeds, and the old farmhouse was fire-eaten and in bad disrepair. The possibility of moving in there might be hopeless.

"Oh, no!" said Cherry. "Not when it's your only chance!" Dr. Hal murmured agreement.

"Well, Mrs. Barker thought I'd better see the old place before counting on it," said Jane. She made an effort to be cheerful. "I hope the three of us can live there, anyway. I'm determined to, even though I haven't seen it yet. We just *have* to make it livable."

So Jane had obtained a leave of absence from her job in New York to come to Iowa, to inspect the farm. She had only three weeks in which to decide whether to keep or sell the old place, figure out whether she and her mother could make it livable, and find out what repairs would cost in money and time. Also, Jane had to explore job possibilities in this area.

"And now I've gone and broken my ankle! With poor Bill just existing from day to day in that hospital, and Mother waiting for word from me," Jane said in despair, "I don't know how I'll ever do all these things in three weeks. I need help. But Mrs. Barker isn't young, and she's kind just to take me in. Floyd is unreliable, so I can't count on him. And I don't know anyone else here."

"You know us," said Cherry. "And through our work we know people who know still others. I think you'll find several persons who will be glad to help you, especially when they hear how urgent your business here is." Jane looked encouraged.

"It's also urgent," Dr. Hal said to Jane, "for you to get well as soon as possible. Your own good health is essential if you're to work out three persons' futures in the next weeks."

"Yes, Doctor," Jane said. She hesitated. "One more thing. Maybe it's not worth mentioning. My mother told me this story as a child, and it haunts me."

The old farm was reputed to hold a secret dating back a hundred years or more. If Jane's great-uncle knew the secret, he never revealed it. Jane said she had asked Mrs. Barker about it, but she had laughed and explained that country folks love fanciful legends and ghost stories.

"Still, I don't understand," Jane said. "Why would there be this persistent family rumor of a secret, if it didn't have *some* basis?"

Dr. Hal smiled. "Maybe a hundred years ago a cricket chirped all night and convinced your great-great-great-aunt that she heard a ghost. Maybe a freak animal was born on that farm, and legend called it the work of the devil."

Jane looked half disappointed. Cherry said:

"I'll tell you what. As soon as you feel able, we'll drive over to the abandoned farm, and we'll see what we can see."

CHAPTER IV

All Kinds of Patients

AT EIGHT O'CLOCK TUESDAY MORNING CHERRY RE-
ported to her office in the courthouse. Dr. Miller was
already there for a conference with her, and was
looking through mail from patients and health agencies.

As they exchanged "good mornings," Cherry's
telephone rang. Doctors in the county were calling
in to request that the county nurse visit certain of
their patients, and gave her orders for nursing and
treatments. Cherry would see these doctors later on,
to report to them. By the time she had answered several telephone calls, she had a long list of visits to
be made that week. In addition, there were letters
from county people requesting help.

"It's going to be a short work week after the holiday," Dr. Hal said to Cherry. "Today I want you to
follow up on the Reed baby and old Mr. Bufford,
and when you can, visit Mrs. Swaybill. Dr. Clark

would like you to see his patient, Dickie Plant, sometime this week. I'll take care of the three urgent calls needing medical consultation myself."

Dr. Hal described the Swaybill and other cases and gave Cherry his orders. She then read records of families she would see today or tomorrow. Four or five thorough home visits was about maximum for a rural nurse in one day, as she had to spend some time driving to her various families.

The county health clerk stopped by to ask when their statistics on the number and types of their cardiac cases would be ready. Dr. Hal picked up his black leather bag, gave a few more instructions, jammed his hat on his head, and left. Five minutes later Cherry gathered up her own list of calls, her nursing kit, the sandwiches Aunt Cora had packed for her, and started off on her own.

She felt a lively sense of freedom, driving along in her small blue car, on her way to take care of patients by herself. She was even able to choose her own dark-blue cotton uniform, and carried in her bag a white coverall apron. A uniform of her own choice was a sign of her independence! Cherry felt as if she had burst out of the four walls of a hospital, with its rigid schedules and strict supervision. For although she had doctors' orders, and also had the regulation "standing orders"—rules to follow in the unlikely event that she could not get in touch with a doctor —she now would rely heavily on her own judgment. "And with no hospital, no clinic, few doctors, for miles around, I'd better do a good job!"

Cherry drove to the Reed farm first, with its small

house and huge red barn. She had been here before, with Miss Hudson, to teach nineteen-year-old Mrs. Reed prenatal care. Now Baby Reed had arrived, and young Dan Reed had brought mother and baby home from the hospital upstate. The new mother needed advice in caring for her baby.

Dot Reed was waiting for the nurse. She could hardly wait to show Cherry her bouncing baby girl. "We named her Ella after my mother. Don't you think she's a big baby? Do all babies cry so much? I'm not sure I'm doing all the right things, the way you taught me—"

Cherry admired Ella, and weighed her in the kitchen scales. "Yes, she's a fine healthy baby," Cherry encouraged the new mother. "Tell me about her crying." Cherry asked other questions, too, checked over the baby and its mother. She explained away some of the worrisome ideas a neighbor had implanted in her. "Babies aren't breakable, you know." Cherry talked to Dot Reed about feeding Ella. Then she demonstrated to Mrs. Reed a simple, safe, and easy method of giving the baby a bath.

"That's fun!" Dot Reed exclaimed as Cherry finished.

"The baby seems to think so, too," Cherry said.

She reminded the new mother to keep a written record of her baby's development, to show to her doctor and also to the nurse on subsequent visits. Then Cherry cleansed her nursing equipment, packed it away in the bag, and said good-by to her two young patients. A good part of the morning had been spent here, but tiny Ella Reed was an important person and getting her off to a healthy start in life was too important a matter to be hurried.

Farther down the road was Bufford's dairy farm. The Buffords were a large, vigorous, hard-working family, Cherry discovered, and at the moment they felt a little impatient with Grandpa. The old man had fallen down the cellar stairs and while, miraculously, he had not broken any bones, he was laid up with cuts and the aftereffects of shock. No one in this busy household had much spare time to spend with him. Besides, his daughter-in-law, Mrs. Sally Bufford, told Cherry in the driveway:

"I tell you, Grandpa is a handful! He won't let me or my girls nurse him—insists the menfolk of the family do it. Well, now, Miss Ames, my husband and boys can't stop their work just to humor him!"

"Maybe we can find other ways to humor him," Cherry said. Dr. Boudineau, who was the Buffords' family doctor, had instructed Cherry on the telephone this morning to see what she could do for the old man's morale.

Mrs. Bufford led her into the house to see the stubborn old man who refused to stay in bed. Cherry got no response from Grandpa until she found he considered himself an expert at raising chickens. Cherry knew as little about chicken farming as she did about astrophysics, but she could and did ask Grandpa's advice on raising chickens. His attitude thawed out considerably. After that, it was a matter of giving a very old person some of the attention he was hungry for. Cherry managed at the same time to check his temperature, examine the cuts on his leg and arm, make sure there was no infection, and apply fresh sterile bandages. He told Cherry he had fallen down the cellar stairs when he was "tryin' to help Sally."

Cherry decided to talk to Mrs. Bufford about those hazardous stairs, and how the family could prevent accidents there and elsewhere on the farm. She urged Grandpa to take life easier, to help chiefly by co-operating—"with the women of the family, too, sir." He grumbled but promised. He even crawled back into bed.

To Sally Bufford, Cherry tactfully suggested: "Can't you find light tasks to keep Grandpa occupied? And can't the men and the youngsters of the family spend a little more time visiting with him? It would help him a great deal. What about a game of cards, or between-meals refreshments, or a radio of his own?" Cherry did not venture to suggest raising chicks in his bedroom, which probably was what Grandpa would have enjoyed most.

By now it was noon. Cherry voted time out for lunch, found a place to turn off the road, and sat down in the grass under a shade tree. While she ate Aunt Cora's sandwiches, she reviewed the morning's visits. A few cars and farm trucks, loaded with produce or cattle, drove past. She was interested to see the Watkins Company door-to-door salesman pass by in his station wagon. The man was well dressed; the car looked trim and professional. Cherry remembered Phoebe Grisbee's saying that farm people were in the habit of buying from door-to-door salesmen. She thought she'd like to do her shopping that way herself.

"Shopping!" Cherry thought. "I shouldn't even *think* about shopping with all the calls I have to make this week!"

On Wednesday Cherry found time to visit Jane Fraser. As Cherry entered the Barker cottage, the parrot in its cage was squawking: "None of your business! None of your business!"

"Mike! Quiet!" Mrs. Barker threw a cover over the cage. The parrot continued to mutter darkly.

"That bird! Repeats everything we say, especially arguments! Just because my son Floyd talked back to me— Sit down, Miss Cherry."

Mrs. Barker sat down, too, and fanned herself. She seemed upset. Jane, she said, was napping.

"I hope the argument Floyd and I had a little while ago didn't disturb her. Honestly, that Floyd! I'm so exasperated with him that if I don't talk to somebody, I'll blow up."

"Talk to me," Cherry said. She was glad to sit and rest for a few minutes, and she did take an interest in Jane Fraser's friend.

"Well, Miss Cherry, you can see for yourself that I work hard around this poverty-stricken place, and I can barely make ends meet. Now wouldn't you think an able-bodied, grown man would do more to help his mother? Or even to help himself? Not Floyd! No, sir, not that lazy hunk." Mrs. Barker fanned herself furiously, then relented. "I don't mean to sound mean toward my only child, *but*—!"

Floyd, she said, had never worked steadily at anything, never married, never undertaken the least responsibility. What he liked to do was to hunt and fish and wander around the countryside. "He aims to enjoy himself." He usually earned just enough cash money to buy gasoline for his jalopy.

"There's no harm in Floyd," his mother said. "It's just that it don't bother him a bit to live in my house and eat his meals here at my expense and leave me with most of the work."

"No, that isn't fair to you," Cherry murmured.

"Precisely! Oh, dear." Mrs. Barker took a long breath. "I told Floyd he's lazy, selfish, shiftless, and not growing any younger. What will become of him when I'm gone? I don't like to nag but I *had* to tell him—"

Outside, a car screeched to a stop. Mrs. Barker sat up straighter in her chair. Mutters of "None of your business!" issued from the covered cage. Then the screen door slammed open and Floyd sauntered in.

He was a lanky, sallow, loose-jointed man in blue jeans and open-necked shirt, in need of a shave, with an amiable and rather blank expression. He was carrying an armful of yellow squash which he set down on the table beside his mother.

"Peace offering, Ma," he said. "Neighbor gave 'em to me for helping him mend his hayrack." He nodded at Cherry and stood waiting to be introduced.

His mother looked scornfully at the squash, as if Floyd ought to contribute more than a few vegetables. Cherry thought Floyd was not much of a man.

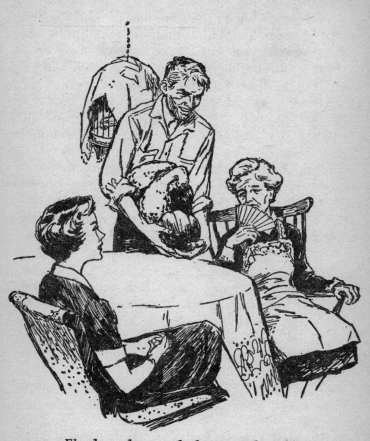

Floyd set the squash down on the table.
"Peace offering, Ma," he said

She heard Mrs. Barker say: "—the new county nurse."

Cherry said hello to Floyd, and decided she must not be prejudiced against him. He probably couldn't help being a weakling. Part of the fault might be his mother's overindulgence. He grinned at Cherry.

"I'll bet from the glint in Ma's eyes that she's been telling you about how I have a gift for avoiding work," he said. His homely face gleamed with humor. "I hope she told you, ma'am, how I'm doing better now."

Mrs. Barker looked slightly ashamed of herself, but said tartly, "A *little* better, son. Only a little."

"It's a good horse that never stumbles, Ma."

"You've been stumbling much of your life," his mother said sadly.

"I don't like work," he said with a wink at Cherry. "Work tires me, Ma."

His mother retorted, "Some men acquire that tired feeling from looking for an easy job."

"Ah, come on, Ma! You know that if I had the time, I'd build us a roadside stand, and you could sell your apples and zinnias to the city folks that drive past. The way a lot of our neighbors do."

"That's all I need!" Mrs. Barker was indignant. "To tend a roadside stand, on top of all else I have to do!"

Floyd shrugged. "Well, if you don't like the idea—" He helped himself from a dish of hickory nuts, and held out the dish to Cherry. "Have some. I gathered 'em last fall, still tasty."

Cherry said, "No, thanks."

Floyd moved good-naturedly toward the door. "Well, nice to meet you. I'll be home in time for supper, Ma."

The screen door slammed again, and Floyd was gone.

Mrs. Barker sighed and then listened. Jane had not been wakened by the racket. "It's a wonder," Mrs. Barker said. "Jane's worn out, that's why. Well, Miss Nurse, I'm glad that at last you've met my son."

The older woman waited for her to make some comment. Cherry did not wish to say anything unkind—she kept to herself her unpleasant impression of Floyd. She thought him shrewder and harder than the bumpkin he appeared to be. She did say that Floyd seemed to have a cheerful disposition.

"Yes, he does." Mrs. Barker looked gratified. "Provided he can be outdoors. He loves the countryside and all living, growing things. I taught my boy all the nature lore I know. And, if I say it as shouldn't, that's considerable. But that's no excuse for him not working, and idling in the woods year in and year out. I told Floyd so. Finally!

"To tell you the truth," Mrs. Barker said, "I never could bring myself to turn my son out of the house. I'd miss him. But recently, Floyd's been so selfish, so irresponsible—just at a time when we need cash money for supplies, and to repair the roof against the winter! Finally, a month or two ago, I told Floyd either he had to earn some money and pay for his keep, or else get out of my house."

"Good for you," said Cherry. "Did it help?"

"Yes, because he actually brings me a little money,

now and then. Floyd's got himself a part-time job at the cannery over at Muir."

"Good." Then Cherry was puzzled. "How can he be at home in the middle of the working day?"

"He works at odd hours, whenever they need him. He won't tell me *exactly* about his hours, or his pay," his mother said. "All he says is—you heard that parrot —'none of your business.' Ah, well. Maybe I expect too much of Floyd."

"Maybe he'll tell you of his own accord, in his own good time," Cherry said.

"Let's hope so."

"Maybe Floyd's improving," Jane said from the doorway. She stood there leaning on her crutches, sleepy and smiling. "Hello, everybody."

"Ah, come on, Ma!" the parrot squawked in answer. "None of your business! Polly want a cracker?"

They all laughed and Mrs. Barker removed the cover from the cage. Mike kept up garbled comments while Cherry checked Jane's cast and her general health.

"You and the ankle are coming along nicely," Cherry said. "At this rate you'll soon be well enough to drive over to see your farm."

"Oh, how soon can you take me?" Jane begged. "Floyd says he'll drive me there, but he keeps putting it off."

"Maybe Saturday morning," Cherry promised. Then she said, "Hello! Hello!" for the parrot's benefit and left.

Once during this first week on her own, Cherry got lost, but the postman came along in his truck and led her part way. On another day her car ran out of gas. Two schoolboys on bicycles brought her a five-gallon can of gas.

Twice during that first week Cherry's nursing calls took her driving past the abandoned farm. She had not paid any special attention to it until now, and thought Jane was going to be discouraged when she saw it. The farm was small, scrubby, gone to seed. Its farthest acres faced on the Missouri River, with Missouri on the opposite shore. The land could be cleared, but the rickety farmhouse was in bad condition. Its second story had been charred by fire and the upstairs windows were broken. However, Cherry thought the stone foundation appeared to be sound, and the downstairs rooms might not have been touched by fire. She remembered a promise she and Dr. Hal had made to Jane—to inquire, as they visited patients, about what local people could make repairs.

One of her pleasantest calls turned out to be at the Swaybill farm. They lived in a big, comfortable house sheltered by oak trees. As Cherry drove into their roadway, she saw a shabby old man at their door, selling something in a basket. Cherry guessed he must be a local peddler; he was a sorry contrast to the professional Watkins Company salesman.

As she came up on the long porch, she was curious to see what he had in his basket. It looked like an assortment of small articles. But the peddler hastily concluded the sale with the person at the door, then slipped away along a side porch. He climbed into an old car and drove away. Cherry had an impression that he was avoiding her. Or was he just in a hurry?

Cherry put the peddler out of her mind when she met the lively Swaybill family. The father and the hired man were working out in the barn, but here in the house were The Big Kids, Clyde and Marge, who were high school students, and The Little Kids, Burt and Betsy, aged six and eight. The entire delegation escorted Cherry upstairs to their mother's room.

Mrs. Amy Swaybill was supposed to be resting. Actually she was up and dressed and shakily hanging curtains. Cherry was horrified, and after introducing herself, stopped her.

"For a person with a heart condition, reaching up is a strain. And you have a sore throat, too. Please lie down now, Mrs. Swaybill."

"Well, I know the doctor would say so, too." Mrs. Swaybill co-operatively went over to the bed. She was a plump, rosy-faced, cheerful woman. Only her slow, weak movements showed that she had developed a chronic heart defect.

"I'm always tired," she told Cherry. "I'm always trying new tonics and remedies in the hopes that they'll build me up. Is there anything you can recommend?"

Cherry sat down facing Mrs. Swaybill. "Yes, I recommend that when the doctor tells you to rest, you really follow his advice. Can't Marge or Clyde hang those curtains for you?"

Cherry talked further with Amy Swaybill on this subject. It became clear that her family was rather thoughtless as far as Mother was concerned. Mother had always done everything for them, and it never occurred to the family to do something for Mother.

"Besides, Miss Ames, I *like* to do for my family! I've always been an active wife and mother. Marge didn't ask me to wash out her best sweater, I offered to—and anyway, Marge does help with the housework."

Cherry saw that she would have to educate the family about the seriousness of allowing Mrs. Swaybill to overtax herself. Amy Swaybill's family could keep her well and out of the hospital.

"Now let's see that sore throat," Cherry said, opening her bag.

She put on her coverall apron, washed her hands, and using a sterile wooden tongue depressor, examined the woman's throat. Cherry was suspicious of what she saw; this might mean a septic sore throat or even diphtheria. Both infections were serious and communicable. This *might* be an epidemic in the making. All Cherry said, however, was:

"Open a little wider, please, so that I can take a throat swab." She would ask Dr. Hal to send it to the hospital laboratory in Iowa City for culture and examination. "That's good, Mrs. Swaybill. You're a very good patient."

Mrs. Swaybill liked Cherry, too, judging from the way she smiled back at her. "You're so quick and gentle, Miss Ames. I wish you'd have a look at the little kids' throats while you're here."

"Yes, I plan to."

Cherry went downstairs and asked Clyde to bring his father and the hired man, Will Hansen, in from the barn. The two men in overalls came in, wiping their hands and faces. Cherry examined everyone's throat. No one but the mother had any infection, she found. She explained about keeping Mrs. Swaybill's dishes separate, and stressed to the family the necessity for giving her more help. The family members listened, half ashamed, eager to do better.

As Cherry got into her car, Amy Swaybill leaned out of her upstairs window. She called weakly:

"Thanks ever so much. Come back soon and stay for supper. There's a new remedy I meant to ask you about—they say it's—" Her words were lost in a rush of wind through the oak trees.

Cherry waved. "You rest, now, or I'll have to tell the doctor on you."

Cherry had a much less pleasant experience when the couple who kept a crossroads grocery store hailed her. They reported an accident at the Hummer place. Cherry drove over at once.

Jacob Hummer and his wife were dour people. Their first question to the nurse was: "Do we have to pay you?"

"My services are free to anyone who can't afford to pay. Let's discuss that later. Let me see your hand, please."

Mr. Hummer looked pale and sweaty. Cherry unwrapped the homemade bandage and found he had a deep cut. Any cut was serious, because it allowed germs to enter the body and cause infection.

"Mr. Hummer, a doctor should treat this wound at once." Cherry explained why. "Who is your family doctor?"

"We don't go to any doctors," Jacob Hummer said.

"We don't hold with too much doctoring. Nature takes care of everything."

"Self-indulgence, to run to a doctor with every ailment!" said his wife. "Needless expense."

"Mr. and Mrs. Hummer," Cherry insisted, "every hour that you neglect this wound, the infection can grow worse. You may be lucky and recover without a doctor's care, or you may not. Let me call a doctor." For it was her responsibility as county nurse to decide when to call a doctor.

"Will he charge us?" Jacob Hummer asked suspiciously.

From the looks of their farm, the Hummers were probably well able to pay. "Wouldn't paying a small fee be better than possibly getting sick and losing working time?" Cherry asked.

"We ain't throwing away money," Jacob Hummer insisted.

Mrs. Hummer angrily told Cherry, "My husband is a very strong man. Nature will heal him. I'm sorry now we called you, if you aim to scare us."

Jacob Hummer held out his torn hand. "You want to treat it for me? Or else I can treat it myself."

Cherry stopped arguing. He did seem to be an unusually strong man. She washed her hands, took out her nursing supplies, and cleansed the wound. She did not see any immediate signs of infection, but these might not be visible yet. She applied a sterile dressing and clean bandage, then took Jacob Hummer's temperature, pulse, and respiration. These were higher than was normal—a danger signal. Cherry said so.

Mrs. Hummer said, "I'll fix my husband some good, strong beef broth and some herb tea. He'll get extra sleep and be all right." The woman squeezed out a smile. "Ah—thanks, Nurse."

"Thanks," said Jacob Hummer. They did not ask her to return.

What a climax to the week's work! Cherry tried to cheer herself up by thinking of her more co-operative patients: Grandpa Bufford, Dot Reed, Mrs. Swaybill and her family, and especially Jane Fraser.

Yet, of all the people she had met this first week as rural nurse, Floyd Barker stood out in her mind. Why? She did not find him particularly interesting in any way. Cherry could not understand why Floyd Barker had made such a forcible impression on her.

CHAPTER V

A Curious Emergency

ON SATURDAY MORNING CHERRY HAD A DATE WITH Jane Fraser. This was the day they were to visit the abandoned farm which Jane had inherited.

"You brought a beautiful day with you," Jane greeted Cherry at the door of the Barker cottage.

"Good morning! You look stronger today," Cherry said. She waited for a garbled echo, but for once the parrot was asleep. The house was quiet. "Where is Mrs. Barker? Gardening?"

"She left bright and early to help a neighbor with some baking," Jane said. "There's going to be a pot-luck supper, a community supper, tomorrow evening to raise funds for the church. All the women are contributing food. If I weren't so clumsy with these crutches, I'd like to go."

"I heard you!" Floyd called, and came in from out-doors chewing on an apple. "Good morning, young ladies."

He stuck the apple core in the parrot's cage. "You

two going over to the old farm this morning?" he asked. They said yes. "Well, don't get your hopes up, Jane. That land's been farmed until it's worn out. And the house! It's only fit for mice and bats to live in, not people."

Jane said indignantly, "I wish you'd stop trying to discourage me."

Floyd wrinkled his forehead. "I'm only telling you facts. I heard the main water pipe is busted. The roof's ready to cave in. Place ain't worth any repairs. Best thing you could do is sell it."

"Please stop interfering!" Jane was growing annoyed. "I don't care what you say, I'm going to try to move in there."

Floyd turned to Cherry. "Miss Cherry, maybe *you'll* listen to me. At least don't go inside the house. Ever since the fire there three years ago, that house is ready to cave in. Be careful."

Cherry nodded and held the screen door open for Jane. As she did so, a framed sampler on the wall caught her eye. Cherry had not noticed it before. It was embroidered in various, faded colors and was dated 1851. It read:

> *If wisdom's ways you truly seek,*
> *Five things observe with care:*
> *Of whom you speak, to whom you speak,*
> *And how and when and where.*

The warning on Mrs. Barker's wall made Cherry uneasy—as if a voice were cautioning her. But that was foolish. . . .

The drive to the abandoned farm took them along

the river road. They passed Riverside Park, passed the woods, and turned into the roadway of the old farm. Or what was left of the private road—it was so thick with weeds that Cherry slowed the car down to a crawl. She drove halfway to the rickety house, which was as close as she could get, parked, and they got out. Even with the sun shining, even with blue sky and blue river, this old place was depressing.

"What a shambles!" Jane exclaimed. "Maybe Floyd is right. I wouldn't know where to begin first to make this place livable."

"Don't let Floyd discourage you," Cherry said.

"Let's explore, shall we?" Jane said. "I know it's dangerous on crutches, but I must have a look."

"Well, at least let me go first," Cherry said.

Cherry went ahead, picking her way, clearing a path as best she could for Jane. The farm grounds were larger than they looked to be from the highway. Half buried by the dense weeds, many other things were growing wild here—tall grasses, goldenrod, haw berries. Bees buzzed around a few gnarled fruit trees and shade trees. Birds swooped from tree to tree, and a bullfrog sang from some pond.

"It's kind of pretty here," Jane said. "At least it's an outdoors place for Bill to live."

Cherry scooped up a handful of earth. It was fragrant, rich black, moist, and firm to the touch. "This soil doesn't look worn out to me," Cherry said. "What a variety of things grow here! I recognize most of them. Do you?"

"Not many. I'm a city girl," Jane said. "Isn't that Indian corn, growing wild?"

As they slowly walked nearer to the house, they came to large patches of a leafy plant. Neither girl had ever seen this plant before. Growing untended, it had spread until it surrounded the house.

"There certainly is a lot of it," Jane said. "What is it?"

"I wonder," and Cherry stooped to take a closer look. "It looks like a sturdy woodland plant."

It grew close to the ground, springing up as tall as twenty inches. Its stalks were covered with several five-leaf clusters and bright crimson berries. Cherry was curious enough to pull up a plant or two. The roots were about as thick as her little finger, three or four inches long, brittle, almost transparent—and, oddly enough, forked.

"The roots look like little men," Jane said. "See, here is the body, here are two arms, and here are two legs."

"You're right," Cherry said. "Think you can walk as far as the house? *Your* house."

She could, in her eagerness, with Cherry helping. Closer up, the house was really dilapidated. The girls could see that once it had been a comfortable farm home. It was small, with many windows, long and narrow and old-fashioned now, but still inviting. They tried to visualize the house with repairs for windows and roof, and a fresh coat of paint.

"White paint," Jane said. "White with dark-green shutters and roof. Stop me from dreaming. Let's go in."

"Well, if it's as unsafe as Floyd said, we'd better

not. But we could at least stand in the main door and look in," Cherry suggested.

There was no front porch, just a stoop, though Jane vaguely remembered a big back porch facing the river. The house itself was pleasantly close to the river. Cherry and Jane stepped up into the front entrance door. The door was unlocked and swung open easily into a long hall.

"Oh, there's the staircase. I remember sliding down the banister!" Jane said. "And just to our left, that's the living room. Or was." Beyond that, down the hall, was the old dining room, and across the rear of the house they could see a kitchen.

The house was so still, as they stood on the threshold and peered in, that they could hear their own breathing. Jane muttered that she wished she knew the century-old secret of this place.

"You wouldn't let a ghost keep you away?" Cherry teased her.

"I'd simply invite the ghost to live with us," Jane said. "Joking aside, there must be some reason why there's a legend or story about this farm. If I could only— Why, what are you doing, Cherry?"

"Sniffing. Don't you smell it?"

A curious sour odor came from somewhere in the house. Cherry could not identify it. At the same time, she noticed how warm the air was in the house. Well, an old, closed-up house, with the mid-September sun beating down on it, could be expected to be hot and smell musty. Except that this sour, moldy odor was not quite the same as dust and mustiness—Cherry sniffed again, trying to locate where the odor came from. It seemed to hang in the air everywhere.

Jane was laughing at her. "You look like a puppy, sniffing in all directions! Can't we go in? . . . Not a good idea? Well, then, Miss Nurse, I admit I'm getting awfully tired."

They agreed it was enough exploring for a first visit. They slowly made their way back to the car. Then they drove on to Sauk. Dr. Hal X-rayed Jane's ankle, which was healing satisfactorily, and Cherry drove her back to the Barkers'. Since she was out in the field anyway, she visited two more patients.

After supper with Aunt Cora, Cherry was so full of fresh air that she could hardly keep her eyes open. She did write a long letter to her nurse friends—all about rural nursing. Then Cherry telephoned her family in Illinois and had a good talk with her mother and father.

Sunday was fun. At church Cherry saw her new friends again, and Dr. Hal. He invited Cherry and Aunt Cora to the potluck supper. Since it was fifteen miles away, and since Cherry and Dr. Hal drove all week at work, Aunt Cora decided they'd go no farther than her own dining table. She appointed Dr. Hal to help her while she made coffee and buttermilk biscuits. Cherry was delegated to bring in the rest of the food, and set the table, not forgetting candles and flowers.

The three of them lingered over supper. Dr. Hal seemed to be enjoying himself. He told them of a discovery he had made about the cave at Riverside Park.

"You remember, Cherry, that you wondered so much what was on the other side of that barrier, deep in the cave? Well, even though I was sure there was nothing, you got me to wondering, too. So I went back there, late yesterday afternoon. Went with Joe Mercer. Took two of us to dislodge that old barn door." He explained to Mrs. Ames how the old door was wedged against, almost into, the walls of the cave. "And what do you suppose Joe and I found?"

"What?" Cherry asked, holding her breath.

"Nothing. A pile of dirt. Just dirt and darkness. Some kids must've dug loose enough dirt to put the old barn door in place. They probably did it to make a hiding place for some game. Joe and I felt foolish, I can tell you! We put the door back as we found it."

"If that's a discovery," Aunt Cora said, "then I'm a ring-tailed monkey."

The first person to tell Cherry the bad news was the highway patrolman. He hailed her to a stop on the highway early Tuesday morning, and braked his car alongside her car.

"'Morning! You're Cherry Ames, the county nurse, aren't you? I'm Tom Richards." He touched his broad-brimmed hat in greeting. He was a strapping, sun-reddened man. "There's some people suddenly taken sick around here, Nurse. Seems they went to the potluck supper—here's their names. One of their youngsters stopped me on the road. They have no telephone to call the county health office."

"Thanks, Officer." Cherry took the slip of paper he handed her. Nichols, R.D. #3. She didn't know them. "I'll go right over there."

"Right. See you again, Miss Ames." The highway patrolman drove off.

Taken sick after the community supper! If one family was stricken, others might be, too. No one had reported sick yesterday, but it took time for an illness to develop. Cherry had left Sauk very early this morning. She stopped at a highway telephone booth and called her office.

"Yes," the clerk said, "several families have phoned in asking for emergency help." The clerk read off their names.

"I'll go see them right away," Cherry said. "Any word from Dr. Miller?"

"He's on his way to the appendicitis case at the Anderson farm," the clerk said. Cherry could make connections with him by telephoning the clerk periodically, as Dr. Miller would do.

At the Nichols' place, Cherry found the father, mother, and the two eldest children in bed, seriously ill. All of them had similar symptoms: fever, extreme weakness, aching back and limbs, running nose, sore throat. Cherry recognized that they had respiratory flu, in its acute stage. These were routine symptoms of respiratory flu.

She did not understand, though, why Mrs. Nichols reported that they all had diarrhea and cramps, and the younger child had been vomiting. Those were not respiratory flu symptoms. Those were symptoms of some *other* type of virus. But what? These patients had flu *and* something else which Cherry could not recognize. The symptoms of the unknown illness—the diarrhea, cramps, and vomiting—had started yesterday.

"Did you call a doctor, Mrs. Nichols?" Cherry asked.

"No, we treated ourselves."

"With what?"

"Oh, just home remedies," the woman said vaguely. Cherry put her vagueness down to her weak, sick state. She asked a few questions about the potluck supper on Sunday. Mrs. Nichols said the room had been crowded and poorly ventilated.

"I guess some people there had colds," the woman said.

"Someone there probably had a flu virus," Cherry said, "and you caught it. I'm going to ask Dr. Miller to come to treat the four of you. Don't try to get out of bed."

Cherry gave first aid. She quickly made the four sick people as comfortable as she could, told the well children to keep away from them, left there, and telephoned for Dr. Miller. Then she drove to the next emergency names on her list.

In some of these families she found flu symptoms. In others she found even more acute flu symptoms plus the unexplained diarrhea and vomiting. Cherry was puzzled. In all the latter cases she noted that the families had "treated themselves with home remedies." *Exactly what home remedies?* Nobody would tell the nurse. They seemed to be evading or too sick to talk.

Among these persons was the forbidding Jacob Hummer. His hand was healing—the man was strong and lucky! But Cherry urgently advised calling a doctor to check his flu infection.

"No!" said Hummer. "Nature will heal me."

"Mr. Hummer, it's necessary! If you won't call a doctor, you can't call me again, either. The rule is that the county nurse can make two home visits to encourage medical care. Only two calls, and no more if the family refuses to call a doctor when the nurse tells them it's necessary."

The Hummers gave in then, reluctant, but frightened by the man's condition. Cherry telephoned in a call for Dr. Miller, and arranged to meet him later that afternoon.

They met and worked together at the Nichols' and the Hummers'. Then they went to the crossroads grocery store, for a conference over a carton of milk. Cherry described her day's cases to Dr. Hal.

"What's this about so many having diarrhea and cramps?" Dr. Hal asked. "Those aren't flu symptoms."

"I think those patients all dosed themselves with some kind of home remedy," Cherry reported, "instead of getting medical help right away."

Dr. Hal frowned. "Find out what the remedy is. I'll inquire, too."

Nobody was willing to tell Cherry what the remedy was. And she could not find out the reason for this silence. One farm woman said she had been advised to "keep mum," but swore she'd heard it effected many cures. Cherry noticed, in the next day or two, that those flu patients who had taken the remedy were sicker than ever. And *not* with flu! The ordinary flu cases were getting well! Dr. Miller, aided by other county physicians, was kept busy treating this emergency. He had a hard time diagnosing the elusive ailment, and when these patients began to recover, it was slowly. On an off-chance, he treated some patients for poisoning; it helped.

"What in the world have they taken?" he said to Cherry. "We *must* find out."

Cherry finally learned something on Friday at the Swaybills' farm. Marge and Clyde, the teen-agers, had attended the potluck supper, and while Clyde had a mild runny nose and sore throat, Marge was acutely sick. She was in bed in her own room. She complained privately to Cherry of terrible cramps.

"I think what did it," Marge said, "was that new patent medicine Mother dosed me with. I wasn't hardly sick until she gave me that stuff yesterday."

Cherry pricked up her ears. "*What* new patent medicine?"

"That herb remedy. Everybody for miles around has been buying it," Marge said. "Mother always thinks this or that new remedy is going to make her stronger, and cure everything."

Cherry went to question Mrs. Swaybill. The hospital laboratory had examined her throat swab of the last visit and found it did not carry any virus; Mrs. Swaybill had just a common, very sore throat. Now Cherry was concerned lest Amy Swaybill catch a further infection from Marge—and she wanted to learn about that new patent medicine.

"Why, it's just a harmless mixture of natural herbs," Mrs. Swaybill answered Cherry's question. "A bowl of herb tea saves you from a fever, they say. So I thought, when Marge began to run a fever, that this new herb medicine sounded good—"

Apparently Mrs. Swaybill relied as much on "natural" remedies as Aunt Cora's friend, Phoebe Grisbee, did. But a patent medicine, even if it included herbs, was quite another matter.

"Where did you get this patent medicine, Mrs. Swaybill?" Cherry asked. Mrs. Swaybill hesitated. Cherry pressed her.

"I bought it from an old door-to-door peddler. He lives around here somewhere. In a shack in the woods, near Muir, I heard. Oh, I can see from the look on your face, Miss Cherry, that you don't think much of these cure-alls! But we've all been buying odds and ends from Old Snell for years, aspirin and shoe laces and vanilla, and herbs and berries in season, and we trust him."

Cherry recalled seeing a shabby old man selling from a basket at the Swaybills' door. She asked Mrs. Swaybill what the patent remedy was like.

"It's a smelly liquid. Nature's Herb Cure is the name. I wish you wouldn't ask questions about it." Cherry inquired why not. "Well, Old Snell asked us to keep quiet. As a friendly favor. Seems this remedy is brand new, and he has only a small amount of it to sell to his steady customers, and he didn't want to offend any other folks who'd ask to buy it if they heard about it."

"I don't like the sound of all this," Cherry said.

"Well, Old Snell *was* a mite uneasy about selling a new product," Mrs. Swaybill admitted. "But I tell you, the stuff is real good! I tried a little bit of it a couple of weeks ago for my weak spells, and it perked me right up! Why, I was so pleased with it, I sent Old Snell to sell some to my cousins across the river, in Missouri. Here's the jar if you want to see it."

Cherry took the jar from Amy Swaybill and studied the printed label. It made claims too numerous and too extreme for Cherry to believe. Its directions for use were crude. The label listed the ingredients only as "natural herbs and preservatives." It gave the manufacturer's name and address as "Nature's Herbs Co., Flushing, Iowa." Cherry asked about that.

"Land's sakes, I don't know the company that makes it," Mrs. Swaybill said.

"Hmm." Cherry remembered Dr. Hal wanted a sample. "May I keep this jar?"

"Surely, if you like. There are only a couple tablespoonfuls left. But you won't get me or Old Snell in trouble, will you? He's only a poor old man trying to make a living. And—and it's helped my cousins in Missouri, too!"

Cherry reported this conversation to Dr. Hal, at her office on Friday evening, and turned the sample over to him.

"So this is what they took," Dr. Hal said. "If only people would consult a doctor, and promptly! If only they wouldn't think they can diagnose their ailments and prescribe for themselves. The claims on the label are fantastic. Listen to this—in fine print."

Hal read aloud: "Cures arthritis, flu, cancer, tuberculosis, falling hair, tiredness—" The young doctor added ironically, "And just about everything that afflicts the human race."

"I never heard of this preparation, did you?" Cherry asked.

Dr. Hal shook his head. "I'll bet you this is the troublemaker. I think we ought to report it to the Food and Drug Administration."

"I thought of that, too," Cherry said.

They discussed what they had better do. Iowa maintained several health agencies to protect its population. However, the peddler had sold the remedy also to Mrs. Swaybill's cousins in Missouri; that constituted interstate commerce and made it a matter for the United States Food and Drug Administration, operating under the Federal Pure Food, Drug, and Cosmetic Act. The job of FDA, the Food and Drug Administration, was to stop the manufacture and distribution of medicines, medical devices, foods, and cosmetics which were unhealthful or impure or worthless or misbranded. FDA could take violators into the federal courts, where they would be liable for heavy fines and jail sentences. FDA thus protected the population against harming themselves.

Honest and responsible manufacturers co-operated with the Food and Drug Administration, checking their new products and label directions with the FDA experts before offering them to the public. But not all manufacturers were honest. That was why the FDA had to be a scientific crime-detection agency. Anyone, a doctor or a druggist or a private citizen, if he had serious doubts about a product, could report it to the FDA. Their inspectors were at work all over the United States, and FDA had branch offices in many cities.

"The branch nearest us," Dr. Hal said, "is in Des Moines. But I wonder whether we oughtn't to notify the state health authorities first?"

"I'll notify Miss Hudson, too," Cherry said. "When are you going to report this awful 'remedy'?"

"Right now," Dr. Hal said, and picked up the telephone. He told the operator that he wanted to put through a call to the State Department of Health in Des Moines. "I know the offices close at five or five thirty, Operator," Dr. Hal said, "but there's probably an emergency line always open."

He and Cherry waited while the call to the state capital went through. It took several minutes. Finally Dr. Hal reached someone, for he said:

"Hello! This is Dr. Hal Miller, county doctor at Sauk, and I want to report a suspicious new medicine." He listened for a while, then said, "Oh. Well, I'm not surprised, I'm calling so late in the day, and now it's the week end. Yes, I'll call again tomorrow morning. . . . No, I don't know too much about this medicine. . . . No, I don't know as much as that, not yet. . . ." He listened again. "That's a good idea. Will do." After another pause, he said, "Thanks very much," and hung up.

"What's 'a good idea'?" Cherry asked.

"Well, you heard that I'm to call back and try to reach the appropriate health officers. The man who talked to me suggested that until a contact can be set up, we get all the information we can about this remedy. Who makes it and where, and what goes into it. Of course they'll make the investigation, but anything we can tell them will save them a lot of time and get this remedy off the market that much faster."

"I see," Cherry said. "What do you want to do with this jar of the remedy, Doctor?"

"I'll keep it. It's evidence to hand over to the health authorities." Dr. Hal picked up the jar as gingerly as if it contained dynamite. "Cherry, I'd like you to be present when I telephone again tomorrow morning. There might be some questions I couldn't answer, but you could."

"I'll be back here first thing tomorrow morning," Cherry said, "Saturday or no Saturday."

"Good. Now I'll walk you home."

CHAPTER VI

Medical Detective Work

ON SATURDAY MORNING HAL AND CHERRY MET IN the county health office at nine o'clock. Hal got on the telephone and stayed there. He held the phone so that Cherry could listen, too.

Hal had difficulty, because it was the week end, in reaching the state health people in Des Moines. He did reach one office and reported the harmful medicine, but was told:

"That's a situation for our State Department of Pharmacy and Narcotics to handle, Dr. Miller. Hold on while I put your call through to them."

A woman secretary answered, and listened while Hal again stated his case. The woman said:

"The person for you to get in touch with is Mr. Henderson, the Director of the Department of Pharmacy and Narcotics. I'm not sure whether I can locate him for you on a Saturday. Let me try, and I'll call you back within an hour."

Cherry and Hal worked with their patients' case records, but even so, the time dragged. At ten o'clock the telephone rang. Hal answered it. The operator said, "Des Moines calling Dr. Miller."

"Hello?" Hal said expectantly. "Mr. Henderson?"

"No, sir, it's the secretary again. I've learned that Mr. Henderson has gone out of town on an inspection trip, and will be home late today. I can give you his home telephone number, if you'd like."

"Yes, I'll take it," Dr. Hal said, and wrote it down. "Thanks. I'll call late this afternoon." He hung up and said to Cherry: "Delays. Can't be helped on a week end, I suppose." He thought for a minute. "You know, Cherry, the State Department of Health man last evening asked me to get all the information I could about this remedy. While we're waiting to reach Mr. Henderson, why don't we ask a laboratory to analyze this concoction?"

"What lab have you in mind?" Cherry asked.

"The hospital lab in Iowa City. Are you free to drive upstate with me? Right away?"

Cherry nodded. Dr. Hal picked up the jar of the remedy that Mrs. Swaybill had given her.

By starting at once and taking short cuts, Dr. Hal and Cherry reached Iowa City by late morning. They parked in front of University Hospital and went directly to its laboratory. Dr. Hal, as a county health officer, knew the chief laboratory technician, Nan Cross, a woman in a starched white coat. He introduced her to Cherry.

"I'm always glad to meet a county nurse," Miss Cross said. "What can the lab do for you, Doctor?"

Dr. Hal Miller handed her the jar of Nature's Herb Cure, with the request that she use only a little of it for biochemical analysis and return the rest to him. The technician nodded, poured some into a container, and gave back the jar. Then Dr. Miller described for Miss Cross the symptoms of his flu patients who had "treated" themselves with the doubtful patent medicine. "Of course I've reported this concoction to the health authorities," he said. While he talked, Cherry glanced around the well-equipped laboratory.

Here on long tables were racks of test tubes, some frothing, some with frozen materials, microscopes, slides, Petri dishes full of cultures. Near the windows were cages of white mice. In the next room was the blood bank. All of this equipment was familiar to Cherry, for no hospital could function without laboratory technicians. These specialists were highly trained in biology, chemistry, and biochemistry, and performed laboratory tests through which physicians could reach an accurate diagnosis.

"I've been treating these special patients not only for flu, but for— Well, the disturbance acted like some kind of poisoning," Dr. Miller was saying to Miss Cross. "Treatments against poisoning have helped so far. It was only late yesterday that Miss Ames was able to obtain this sample of the cure-all."

"I'll run tests on white mice," Miss Cross said. "We'll study how this patent medicine affects them, since, as you know, mice and men have the same physical make-up. I'll give the medicine to mice which I'll infect with flu virus, and I'll also give it to healthy mice, as a control test." She added, "It will take a few days for results to develop."

"This patent medicine produces discomfort fast," Dr. Miller said. "I urgently need your reports so I'll be able to prescribe the most effective treatment for patients, and also I'd like to report the results of the tests to the health authorities. Can't you start the tests right now and let us have an answer by Monday or Tuesday?"

The lab technician bit her lip, figuring. "I'll speed things up, Doctor. As soon as I have some answers, I'll phone you or Miss Ames at your county health office."

"That's fine. Thanks very much," Dr. Hal said. "Is there a chemist here today?"

Miss Cross said no, but there was a commercial chemistry laboratory in town, Greer's, which the medical personnel, food processors, local druggists, and the university-trained farmers relied on.

Greer's Laboratories was in an office building. Dr. Thomas Greer, a tall, graying man wearing a lab coat and rubber gloves, stopped his experiment to talk with Dr. Hal and Cherry. Cherry felt at home in the quiet laboratory with its racy odors and its tables and shelves piled with big pieces of equipment, racks, flasks, reference books, and typed reports.

"A breakdown of the elements in this patent medicine?" the chemist said, as Dr. Hal handed him the jar. He unscrewed the top and sniffed its contents. "What do you think is in this mixture? After all, this could be any one of a thousand different things."

Cherry remembered that the peddler who sold the stuff lived in the woods; he picked berries and herbs, and sold those, too. She recalled Phoebe Grisbee's and Amy Swaybill's faith in herbs as cure-alls.

"Mightn't the remedy contain some sort of herb that grows wild in these parts?" Cherry suggested. "As one of the ingredients?"

"The label does mention herbs," Dr. Greer said. "Well, we'll test for an herb. My two assistants are off today—if either of you'd like to help a bit."

"We're rusty," Dr. Hal warned him. But Cherry said, "Helping with an analysis is exciting—like detective work!"

The chemist smiled at her. "Exactly how I feel, too. Let's start."

First Dr. Greer made a litmus-paper test. Then he took a clean glass test tube, poured what was left of Nature's Herb Cure into it, handed the jar back to Hal, and placed the test tube on a Bunsen burner with its blue-violet flame. Cherry sniffed as the liquid bubbled and gradually separated into its component elements. It certainly was smelly. Dr. Greer pointed out a sediment which settled at the bottom of the test tube.

"We'll set up an experiment with the sediment," the chemist said. First he examined it under the microscope. "I think this is panacin." Then he mixed it with another chemical, to see how it would react, and tried it with other catalysts. "Yes, this is panacin," Dr. Greer said. "It's the main constituent of this patent medicine."

Cherry and Dr. Hal were not sure what panacin

was. Dr. Greer explained that it was an oily, gluey substance derived from the *Panax* plant. He said it could slightly soothe irritated mucous membrane. It also had a slightly stimulating effect as a tonic.

"Why don't you look it up?" the chemist said, and pointed out a copy of *The Merck Index of Chemicals and Drugs* on the bookshelf. This was a standard reference book giving a list of drugs and chemicals.

"I'd like to look it up," Cherry said, and took down the heavy volume. She turned to "ginseng" and read that panacin is derived from the five-leaf (quinquefolium) *Panax* or ginseng plant. The chemical constituents of the plant are panacin, sugar, starch, mucilage— Cherry skipped over other ingredients in the long list. She read that *The Pharmacopeia of the United States of America* had recognized ginseng 1840–1880 as an aromatic bitters with a mildly soothing and stimulating effect. But at present, and since about 1906 when the Federal Pure Food and Drug Act was enacted, ginseng had no official value. *It's like herb tea,* Cherry thought, *nearly worthless as a drug.*

Then she consulted a botany book and read in surprise:

"American *Panax* or ginseng, a perennial, is a small, leafy, originally woodland plant. It is native to the United States; it also grows in China. In early days in America, ginseng hunters, even a century ago, found large patches of ginseng where for hundreds of years the plant had grown untouched." She went on reading. "Ginseng is now rare and little known. Some wild patches can still be found, grow-

Dr. Greer poured the remedy into a test tube

ing in the temperate-weather zone around the Mississippi River, particularly in Illinois and Iowa."

Particularly in Iowa! "Its stalks carry five-leaf clusters. In September it has bright crimson berries. It has a forked root like a human figure, two to four inches long, translucent and brittle. Ginseng grows wild and can be transplanted, or it can be cultivated. Ginseng requires very little care or nurture."

Why, this was the plant growing in profusion at the abandoned farm! The distinctive plant neither she nor Jane had ever seen before! The plant which had been common enough a hundred years ago— *A century ago,* Cherry thought. *The secret of the old farm dated back a hundred years or more.* Cherry turned the page and found a detailed pen-and-ink drawing of the *Panax* or ginseng leaves and root. She recognized it as exactly the same plant! She had never seen ginseng growing anywhere else around here. Nor had Dr. Hal, when she excitedly asked him.

The chemist was busy with paper and pencil, reconstructing the formula of the patent medicine, muttering, "Traces of albumen." He looked up and noticed Cherry's excitement. "Have you found something interesting, Miss Ames?"

"Yes, I have!—in this book—I mean, especially at an abandoned farm near Sauk," she sputtered. It took her a moment to calm down, and explain to Dr. Hal and the chemist.

They agreed her discovery was important. The ginseng that went into the patent medicine might very well be the same ginseng growing at the abandoned farm. If so, they had their first lead toward finding the irresponsible or dishonest manufacturer of Nature's Herb Cure.

"But look at this address," Dr. Hal objected. He held up the jar and read: " 'Manufactured by Nature's Herbs Company, Flushing, Iowa.' Is Flushing near here? I never heard of it."

Dr. Greer, a native Iowan, had never heard of Flushing, either. "Never mind where the place is. Ginseng is uncommon. The ginseng used in this remedy might be grown around Sauk, and shipped to Flushing."

"Dr. Greer," Cherry asked, "if I were to go to that old farm this afternoon and bring you back a ginseng plant today or tomorrow, how soon could you analyze it? To find out for certain whether it has the same ingredient, the panacin, that you just found in this patent medicine—"

"I could analyze it Monday morning," the chemist said. "All I'll need will be the root."

"I'll bring it late today or tomorrow."

Dr. Greer obligingly gave her his home address in case the laboratory was closed. They completed the day's business with the chemist, paid and thanked him, and left.

On the drive back to Sauk, Cherry and Dr. Hal stopped for late lunch at a highway diner. Dr. Hal decided to notify all the other local doctors at once of what he and Cherry were beginning to find out.

"I'd like to tell Jane what's up," Cherry said. "It's her farm that's involved."

"That *may* be involved," Dr. Hal corrected her. Cherry smiled. "Yes. Just the same, I think she should be told. It's her property. Would you mind, Hal? And would you mind if I took Jane to the old farm with me this afternoon?"

Dr. Hal said he had no objection. He drove Cherry back to Sauk, to her aunt's house, and went off to his patients. Cherry said a quick hello to Aunt Cora, explained she was at leisure that afternoon, and dashed off for the garage and her own car.

"At leisure?" Aunt Cora called after her. "I never saw anyone so busy in my life!"

CHAPTER VII

A Theft and Some Answers

CHERRY FOUND JANE FRASER SITTING IN THE SUNNY
yard with Mrs. Barker. They were slicing vegetables
for supper, holding a pan apiece in their laps. Cherry
heard Floyd whistling in the house.

"Jane, would you like to come for a little drive?"
Cherry asked. "Would you, Mrs. Barker?"

Emma Barker was too busy, but urged Jane to go.
"Floyd!" she called. "Bring Jane's sweater, will you?
She and Miss Cherry are going riding."

In a minute or two Floyd sauntered out carrying
Jane's sweater. "I'll go along with you," he said. "I
just feel like a ride."

"No, sir. Sorry, but you're not invited this time,"
Cherry said quickly. Perhaps a shade too quickly.
The investigation of ginseng and the remedy was
none of Floyd's business. "This is an all-feminine
party."

He shrugged and—when his mother prompted

him—helped Jane maneuver her crutches as she got into Cherry's car. The two girls drove off.

"This is a pleasant surprise," Jane said. "I thought you'd be busy even on a Saturday afternoon."

"I *am* busy. This drive has a purpose. Jane, can you keep a secret? It concerns your farm, in part—or it may."

Cherry told her all that she and Dr. Hal had discovered so far. Jane, with her nutritionist's training in biology, chemistry, and biochemistry, understood what Cherry was telling her. She was shocked at the possibility that their neighbors were endangering their health with the so-called remedy.

"We've all heard about that Nature's Herb Cure," Jane said. "I thought it might be harmless, or worthless at the worst. But I never suspected it might be dangerous. Do you suppose there's any chance that the ginseng growing on my farm—?"

"I'm afraid it's a possibility, Jane."

They turned in at the abandoned farm and parked the car. Cherry got out alone. She walked to the edge of the big ginseng patch and pulled up eight or nine plants by the roots. Jane watched as Cherry examined the roots to make sure she had an adequate, average sampling. She discarded two rotted roots, and picked others.

"How quiet and lonely it is here!" Jane called from the car. "I hear that bullfrog croaking."

"Must be a pond or stagnant water around here," Cherry answered. "That's where your bullfrog lives."

Stagnant water, probably with flies or mosquitoes

breeding in it and in the dirt of an abandoned house. The place needed a thorough disinfecting, scrubbing, painting, before it would be fit to live in —not to mention the fire-eaten second floor. She wandered closer to the house, looking for any bare spots where someone else had pulled up ginseng plants and roots. The patch grew so thickly that she could not tell.

Cherry returned to the car and put her armful of plants and roots on the back seat. She noticed that Jane looked troubled.

"I wish this ginseng plant weren't growing on my farm," Jane said. "If someone is gathering this plant to make that medicine—well, it's rather frightening. I have enough problems, without this additional worry."

Cherry said, "Maybe whoever is helping himself to this wild patch of ginseng—*if* anybody is—doesn't know that a new owner has this farm now."

Jane was still uneasy on the drive back. To cheer her up, Cherry told her how she and Dr. Hal had been inquiring on their rounds—among patients, among acquaintances, in Sauk, at the Iowa City hospital—about a nutritionist's job for Jane. One or two leads were shaping up. Jane was encouraged.

"If only this ankle would hurry up and heal," she said with a sigh. Cherry had to help her out of the car at the Barker cottage. Jane went up the path. "Mrs. Barker loves to have company. Have you a few minutes to come in and visit?"

"On a Saturday afternoon, yes, thanks."

The old lady put aside her chores and came into

the little sitting room to chat. If Floyd was around, he did not intrude on them. Mike, the parrot, was asleep hanging upside down.

Mrs. Barker wanted to have a tea party, but the two girls would not let her bother. Cherry admired the old sampler on the wall.

"My great-grandmother embroidered it," Mrs. Barker said. "I still darn socks the way she taught my grandmother. I used to do embroidery, too. But fine needlework is a lost art nowadays—though there'll surely be some nice patchwork quilts on display at the county fair."

They talked about going to the fair next month— Jane could meet local people there and ask about repairing the old house. Besides, the fair was a gala event.

After half an hour, Cherry said she must go. Emma Barker was so disappointed that Cherry explained:

"I want to stop in to see Mrs. Reed and her baby. Then, too, I promised my aunt to buy a bushel of apples at the crossroads grocery store. She likes their Rome Beauties."

Cherry did not add that she also hoped to have time to drive to Iowa City with the ginseng roots for the chemist.

At Dot Reed's she found mother and baby in fine shape, and left some baby-care pamphlets. Then Cherry drove on to the grocery store at the crossroads. Because it was a Saturday afternoon, a large number of cars and station wagons were parked out in front and the store was crowded. Cherry visited with several people until it was her turn to be waited on. The grocer carried the bushel basket of apples out to Cherry's car for her.

As Cherry opened the car door for the grocer to put the apples in the back seat, she gave a little cry. The ginseng plants and roots were gone!

"What's the matter, miss?" the grocer asked.

"Something's been stolen from my car! Nothing valuable, but—but I never thought to lock the car."

"That's a real mean trick," the grocer said. "Anything I can do to help?"

Cherry thanked him and said no. He went back to his customers. For a moment or two Cherry simply stood there, she was so surprised. Who would steal the ginseng samples from her? Someone who did not want the county nurse to find out too much? Someone who did not want the medical people to link the ginseng plant with the dubious medicine?

Had someone trailed her and Jane to the abandoned farm, and observed her picking the ginseng? She hadn't noticed anyone. Unless someone lurking inside the old farmhouse had watched her—then followed her— Cherry felt a momentary terror but controlled herself. She had seen no one follow her from the farm.

Well, then, at what point had the unknown person stolen the ginseng from her car? She had parked the car, unlocked, at three places—here in the crowded space in front of the grocery store, briefly in front of Dot Reed's house, and before that, at Mrs. Barker's. She'd been at the Reeds' on a wide-open stretch of highway too short a time for the theft to have occurred there. She'd been parked longest—half an hour—outside Mrs. Barker's cottage, when she brought Jane home and stayed to visit. That would have given the thief ample time to help himself to the ginseng.

Floyd! Floyd might still have been around the Barker place during that half hour, and out of sheer nosiness and mischief, he could have poked into her car. That might be his malicious retort to not being included in her and Jane's drive.

Or—*if* Floyd was the thief—did he have some other motive for taking her samples of ginseng?

"But the thief must know I can go back to the old farm and pick more ginseng," Cherry thought. Maybe the theft was a subtle warning that she was being watched. Cherry recalled her first impression of Floyd Barker—he appeared to be a not-very-bright country bumpkin, but she had sensed something hard and tricky in him.

On the other hand, the thief need not necessarily be Floyd at all. She'd been inside the grocery store for a good fifteen or twenty minutes. The thief could have taken the plants during that time. So many possible answers!

As she reached into the back of the car to steady the basket of apples, she noticed something on the car floor. It was a ginseng root. Good! Here was one root the thief had overlooked or dropped. She still had a sample!

Cherry telephoned Aunt Cora from the grocery store that she didn't know how late she would be home that evening, and not to wait for her for supper. Then she turned the car around and headed for Iowa

City. It was dark by the time she got there and left the root for Dr. Greer. It was dark and chilly on the drive home to Sauk. No one followed her and nothing untoward happened.

However, the first thing she did on reaching home was to telephone Dr. Hal and tell him what had happened. He was disturbed about the theft, too.

"You've had quite a day," he said. "Rest yourself tomorrow. I'll come over and buy you a soda. Don't worry, now. We should have the laboratory reports by Monday or Tuesday, if we're lucky."

"Did you reach Mr. Henderson?" Cherry asked.

"Not yet, but soon. I talked to his wife, and she said he phoned that he'll be working on this same inspection job all evening, and will be home tomorrow morning," Hal said. "So I'll call him at his home tomorrow morning. It's progress."

Hal kept his word about coming over to treat her to a soda on Sunday afternoon. And he had encouraging news. The head of the State Department of Pharmacy and Narcotics agreed with Dr. Hal that action should be taken immediately to investigate the troublemaking remedy. He would try to send an inspector tomorrow, Monday. At the moment all of his inspectors were out on field trips, but he would make every effort to send a man by tomorrow.

"Good," said Cherry. "That's a relief."

"I also told Mr. Henderson," Dr. Hal said to Cherry, "that Snell is selling the remedy in both Iowa and Missouri, that makes it interstate commerce —so the Federal Food and Drug Administration would probably be interested in this case. Mr.

Henderson said he'd take that factor into consideration, and maybe he'll decide to call in the Food and Drug people. But, in the meantime, he'll try to have an inspector here in Sauk tomorrow." Hal sighed. "I feel relieved, too. I'd feel still more satisfied if I could see those lab reports."

Monday noon, on her lunch hour, Cherry telephoned from the field to her office in Sauk.

"Just a moment," said the clerk. "Dr. Miller is here, and he wants to talk with you."

Hal's voice came on. He sounded excited.

"Cherry, I have the lab technician's—Miss Cross's —report. She just telephoned it in. Wow, this is a bombshell! Listen to this!"

He read the report and Cherry could scarcely believe it, it was so appalling. First, the patent medicine was worthless as a cure. In the tests run on the flu-infected mice, giving them the patent medicine did not check the flu in the least—instead it made them sicker, inducing diarrhea and vomiting. Second, the patent remedy was dangerous. In the tests run on well mice, the patent medicine made many of them sick.

Miss Cross has discovered that the patent medicine was contaminated by live bacteria—by a form of *Salmonella* bacteria, which were communicated from chickens, usually from dirty eggshells contaminated by chicken manure. It was the bacteria, not the harmless ginseng, which made the mice—and Dr. Hal's and Cherry's patients—so very sick.

said, "I remember that the chemist men-
...men, when he was figuring out the for-
...that concoction."

...n't remember it," Dr. Hal answered. "Well,
...nufacturer puts eggs into that remedy, along
with ginseng. And he put in the filth on the eggshells
at the same time!"

"...bacteria!" Cherry said. "How can anyone
"Anything to make money," Hal said dryly.

Cherry remembered Mrs. Swaybill saying she
had taken a little of the concoction about two weeks
ago and found it mildly stimulating. Well, that particular batch two weeks ago apparently hadn't been
contaminated.

Cherry was angry, and concerned for her patients.
She knew Dr. Hal was angry, too. They agreed to
advise their patients and acquaintances to throw
away the so-called remedy.

Within the hour Dr. Greer telephoned in his report, too. Cherry, checking back again by telephone
to the office, had the clerk read it to her.

The chemist's report stated that he had analyzed
the ginseng root from the deserted farm. It was
chemically identical with the ginseng which was the
chief constituent of the patent medicine. That is,
probably someone was using the ginseng from the
deserted farm to compound this patent remedy.

There was only the remotest chance, Cherry re-
flected, that the ginseng came from some other
source—for ginseng was rare. Around here it grew

only on the old farm. Unless there was a patch growing in Flushing, Iowa, where the said the remedy was made?

Out of curiosity that afternoon, between visits to patients, Cherry went to the library in one of the rural high schools and hunted for Flushing on a detailed map of Iowa. She could not find it on a label had nor in the state directory, nor in any. There was no such place — lied to cover up the fact lied about this point, too—lied to cover up the fact that the patent medicine was being made right around here, to divert suspicion. Cherry remembered the sour odor and the dirt in the abandoned farmhouse. What would Hal think when she told him all this!

Cherry resumed her visits to her patients. By five o'clock, she thought, "The state inspector must be in Sauk by now. I wonder whether he's with Hal at the county health office, or at Hal's office?"

But on returning to Sauk, she found the county health office empty. At Dr. Hal's office she found him alone, and on the telephone again. He looked worried.

"All right, Operator, I'll wait," he said, and then to Cherry, "Sit down."

She sat down and pulled off her hat. "Where's the State Food and Drug inspector?"

"He couldn't come today. The arrangements fell through," Dr. Hal said wearily. "Yes, Operator? . . . All right. I'll wait for you to call me back."

Cherry stared. "Have you been on the telephone all afternoon?"

"For the last hour and a half," Dr. Hal said. He stretched and leaned back in his desk chair. "Mr. Henderson called me late this afternoon to say that he's been trying all day to locate an inspector for us, but all of his inspectors are still busy and vitally needed on their present investigations. He's short one man, too. He won't have a man to send us for another day or two."

"But we mustn't wait," Cherry said. "Not after what those lab reports showed!"

"I told Mr. Henderson about the lab reports," Dr. Hal said. "And rather than wait another day or two for a state man, I asked Mr. Henderson to call in the Food and Drug Administration. You know the federal people have a large staff and district offices all over the United States—much bigger than state facilities. Well, Mr. Henderson said by all means let's call in the FDA people at once. In fact, he said, 'This interstate case sounds like too much for us to handle. It sounds like a case for the federal authorities.' He wants us to keep him advised, though. He offered to report to the Food and Drug district office in Des Moines for me, but I thought it would be better—more direct—if I make the federal contacts myself."

"And that's why you're on the phone," Cherry said. "How much progress have you made?"

"Well, I reached the United States Food and Drug people in Des Moines, and told a couple of intermediary persons that I want to make an urgent report. They're going to put me in touch with the right official. That's what I'm waiting for right now."

The phone rang. Hal answered. The operator said that the United States Food and Drug district office in Des Moines was on the line. A man's voice came on. Hal held the phone so that Cherry, leaning close, could hear, too.

Hal gave his name and stated the situation—sale of a worthless, contaminated medicine—a peddler selling it in two states, that is, in interstate commerce —selling it on the basis of false claims.

"That constitutes a violation, doesn't it?" Hal asked.

"It certainly does!" the FDA man said. He gave his name: Fred Colt. "Will you describe the medicine?"

The young doctor reported what the two laboratory studies had revealed. He stated the effects of Nature's Herb Cure on his and other doctors' patients.

"That's typical. We had a case like that in Kansas City," Mr. Colt said. "The manufacturer was sentenced to two years' imprisonment. Who makes this Nature's Herb Cure?"

"We don't know. But there is a peddler whom we suspect in the neighborhood." Hal discussed this point, briefly.

"Have you a sample for us? . . . No? . . . Just the empty jar? The FDA man sounded concerned. "We'll need a sample. Of course it's Food and Drug's job to get it, but it would be a great help to us if you could give us a lead where to find one. We can't prosecute or take any action without a sample. We can't even stop the sale of the medicine."

"Well, sir," Hal said, "could you possibly send an

inspector here right away? Our county nurse, Cherry Ames, discovered that a lot of people are taking this so-called cure on the word of an ignorant, backwoods peddler. He claims this herb stuff can cure practically anything."

"One of those herb quacks, eh?" Mr. Colt said. "They can do a great deal of harm. Had a case last month where a woman died after taking one of those 'remedies.' All right, Dr. Miller. We'll send a Food and Drug inspector immediately. Give me your phone number and address." Hal did so. "Good. We want to send someone experienced in handling this type of case. We'll check and see whom we can find to send. We'll phone you tomorrow, as early as possible, as soon as we know."

"Thanks!" Hal hung up.

Cherry glanced at her wrist watch. "Will they find anyone so late in the day?"

"These men don't keep any hours," Hal said. "I understand that in an emergency they work around the clock, and on Sundays, and anywhere they're needed. That's why it's difficult to reach these inspectors—they're so often out on field trips."

"Well," said Cherry, "patience is a virtue. All we can do is see what tomorrow brings."

~~~~~~

CHAPTER VIII

A House with a Secret

"ONE GOOD THING," DR. HAL POINTED OUT TO CHERRY early the next morning at the county health office. "At least now I know precisely how to treat the ill effects caused by Nature's Herb Cure."

He snorted at the name. He had already telephoned all the other county doctors about his and Cherry's medical investigation, and had notified the appropriate Iowa state health agencies. Cherry had already telephoned Miss Hudson, her nursing supervisor, to report this matter.

"Food and Drug likes to have a sample of whatever is being reported," Dr. Hal said. "If only we could direct a Food and Drug inspector to the manufacturer — But we can't, because we don't know who makes this dangerous stuff, or where."

Cherry realized that the laboratory technician and the chemist had used up all of the small sample she and Dr. Hal had brought.

"We'll have to ask our patients for some of the remedy," Cherry said. "I'm not optimistic about that." Only Mrs. Swaybill had co-operated before.

"Do your best. At the same time," Dr. Hal reminded Cherry, "tell them to throw the stuff away. Tell them to pass on the warning."

Hal went back to his private office to wait for the Federal Food and Drug people's call. Cherry started out on her nursing rounds.

She had a long list of calls today, and a hard time. As soon as she told several patients and their families that Nature's Herb Cure was dangerous, they closed up like clams. They had been evasive about the new medicine before; now they were doubly so. Cherry could not win their confidence. She wondered whether it was because they were loyal to the old peddler—or because they would not admit they had been gullible in buying a quack remedy— or because they trusted in supposedly natural remedies—or a combination of all of these reasons? In any case, Cherry could not persuade a single person to let her have his or her jar of Nature's Herb Cure.

"We used it up."—"If it's no good, what do you want it for?"—"Why, I never bought any in the first place!"

As a last resort, she stopped in at the Swaybills'.

"I'm mighty sorry, Miss Cherry," said Mrs. Swaybill, "but I already gave you all I had."

"Would your cousins just across the river in Missouri have any left?"

"They were over here Sunday to see us, and they said they accidentally spilled what they had of it.

I'll tell you what, though! If Old Snell comes around, I'll buy some more and keep it for you."

Cherry was afraid, though, that as the doctor's warning against the remedy spread, the peddler would hear of it and would stop selling the remedy. She wondered about the peddler. Everyone for miles around considered Old Snell an honest person to trade with. But if he were honest, he would not sell it, now that a warning was abroad.

Cherry worried about something else, later that day. Although her patients denied it, she saw the same unmistakable symptoms again—these persons had taken Nature's Herb Cure. These were *new* patients—all living in one area—*new* customers of Snell's. The racket was spreading!

As she treated these patients, Cherry warned them not to use the "remedy," to throw it away. Two persons, realizing it had made them sick, had already done so. The others might still have some, but Old Snell must have persuaded them to be silent.

On her last home visit that day, a woman argued when Cherry emphatically warned her not to take the preparation. But she was sick enough to consent to let Cherry call Dr. Miller. Then Cherry said:

"Would you do me a favor? Would you give me, or sell me, your jar of Nature's Herb Cure?"

The woman's face tightened. "I haven't got any left."

"Well, then," Cherry tried again, "will you tell me when you bought it from Old Snell?"

"Well, I swan! Why are you so inquisitive about him? He's only a poor old fellow trying to make a living. He told me you and the doctors aim to drive him out of business. All because you can't stand his competition. Says the medicine's got a secret, exclusive formula that you haven't got, and you're jealous and afraid of this new discovery. Says you're persecuting him, and it's not fair."

Cherry gasped. "Is that the story he's spreading? Let me tell you the truth—" and she gave the woman the facts. "Now, please tell me, when did you buy that quack medicine from Old Snell?"

"Oh, a few days ago—maybe day before yesterday. I don't rightly remember."

Cherry had seen the peddler only that one time, slipping away from the Swaybills' house. But, according to this patient, he *was* still selling the cure-all.

Cherry felt gloomy all day Tuesday over the impossibility of locating a second sample. The only encouraging thing today was that the ordinary flu cases now were well or nearly well.

By the time Cherry finished with her visits, it was late and a chilly rain was starting.

"I'd like a cup of hot tea before I drive back to Sauk," Cherry thought. "I'm not far from Mrs. Barker's. I'll go throw myself on her doorstep."

The Barker door opened to Cherry's knock. Jane admitted her.

"Ssh!" Jane said. "Mrs. Barker has a cake in the oven. Walk lightly."

"And don't you slam the door," Cherry said. She walked in on tiptoe. The parrot squawked at her. "I was hoping for a cup of tea, but if Mrs. Barker is busy in the kitchen—"

"Can you wait for the tea?" Jane asked. "To tell you the truth, I need to talk to you privately. About Floyd. I have some doubts about him."

"So have I, though I may be blaming the wrong person. Remember, Jane, we picked some ginseng roots last Saturday afternoon— Floyd isn't here to overhear, is he? Well, then—"

Cherry moved the parrot out of earshot. Then she told Jane Fraser about the theft of the ginseng roots from her car. She also told, in confidence, what the laboratory technician and the chemist had found out about Nature's Herb Cure.

"How awful!" Jane exclaimed. "Exploiting sick people!" They discussed the laboratory findings. Then Jane said:

"What I learned isn't as definite as your news but it—it makes me uneasy. You see, Floyd's comings and goings are at such irregular hours that even his mother has noticed."

"How can he hold a job at the cannery at that rate?" Cherry asked. "What *does* he do at the cannery?"

"Floyd refuses to say," Jane answered. "He's secretive and resentful of his mother's questions. Yesterday, after Floyd had left for work, Mrs. Barker wanted to ask him a question—something about where he had put the shovel for the cellar coalbin. She called him up at the cannery," Jane told Cherry. "And what do you think? He isn't working there. He never has worked there. The people who do the hiring at the cannery never even heard of him."

"Then where—" Cherry stopped short. She had started to say: *Then where does Floyd get the money he now gives his mother occasionally?*

But Jane said: "Oh, that's enough about Floyd! We have more important things to worry about. You know, Cherry, I was thinking that if we could clear out these big beds of ginseng—"

A knock on the front door interrupted Jane. "Goodness, you'll never get your tea!" she said, rising.

There was a flurry of activity as Jane and Mrs. Barker reached and opened the door together. Mr. Brown, a neighbor, had come to talk to Jane about repairing the water pipes in the old farmhouse. Mrs. Barker and Cherry went into the kitchen.

"I heard Jane say you wanted a cup of tea," Mrs. Barker said. Cherry asked her not to bother. "Oh, I'll have one with you, Miss Cherry. I can do with a hot drink after an afternoon's baking."

Emma Barker's kitchen was a warm and cheerful place to be on a rainy afternoon. It was filled with the fragrance of butter and sugar, and of flowering begonia in pots on the window sills. Cherry admired the copper teakettle, and asked about a row of books on a shelf.

"Those are cookbooks," Mrs. Barker said. "Some of them belonged to my mother, and some to my grandmother." She opened one for Cherry, to show her the recipes handwritten in faded ink.

Cherry read aloud: "Take three pounds of unsalted

butter, three pounds of fine white sugar, a dozen and a half freshly laid eggs— Why, that would make enough cake to feed several families!"

"People used to have big families," Mrs. Barker put the cookbook back on the shelf. "Sit down, child, and let's have our tea. I don't refer to these old books much. They're just curiosities nowadays."

Her hospitable hostess took a pan of cookies from where they were cooling on the sink, and offered them to Cherry.

"Speaking of curiosities," said Mrs. Barker, "I have one old book that'd specially interest you, since you're a nurse. It's called *The Compleat Housewife*. The title page says it was published in 1753, in England, and it's been handed down in our family. It has six hundred recipes for cooking and remedies."

"Remedies?" Cherry repeated. This might be a find! She hid her excitement.

"Would you believe it, my copy is the *fifteenth* edition! Some country folks still use those recipes for nourishing dishes and medical herbs and simple home remedies. For myself I'd rather use a doctor and up-to-date scientific medicine. Still, people who live close to the soil know some sensible ways of living. Same as the animals know what's good for them. Let's see where that old formula book is."

Mrs. Barker rummaged through the volumes on the shelf. She grew flushed. "That's peculiar, I can't find it. I always keep it right here."

She hunted through other shelves and drawers. She was so disconcerted that Cherry helped her search. The old book did not turn up.

"Well, never mind," Mrs. Barker said at last, sitting down again at the kitchen table. "Floyd probably knows where it is, he may have borrowed it. I can't imagine that anyone else'd take it. He's always looking up the names of the green things he finds in the woods and fields. A real countryman."

Countryman, indeed! Cherry recalled the sour odor in the deserted farmhouse. Was Floyd compounding a medicine there? Where *did* Floyd get the money he gave his mother now and then? It was easy to guess: he might have a stake in the patent medicine. He and the old peddler might be in this racket together—a racket which centered around the abandoned farm.

Cherry was convinced of one thing: that Mrs. Barker herself was in no way involved. She was such a straitlaced, hard-working woman, it would never even enter her mind that Floyd could be connected with such an evil scheme.

"You know, Miss Cherry," Mrs. Barker was saying, "in olden days, a farm without a few medicinal herbs growing would have been as unheard of as a barn without a barn cat or a well without a pail. People *had* to treat themselves, because doctors and medicines were a rarity."

"Tell me about this old formula book," Cherry said. "What about the homemade remedies?"

The old lady rattled off the names of several time-honored favorites: mustard plaster; sassafras tea; asafetida worn in a bag around your neck for a spring tonic; ginseng to both soothe and stimulate.

"I'd say these things do good as far as they go—"

"What do you think about ginseng?" Cherry asked.

"Oh, I don't hold much with ginseng," Mrs. Barker said. "Mostly people used to value it because the root is forked and shaped like a human figure, but that's only legend, superstition. Ginseng just makes you feel better temporarily. So would a cup of hot tea. I do believe there's at least one ginseng formula in my book! You grind up the dried ginseng root into a powder, and then you add—let me see— Oh, dear, I forget."

Cherry kept silent. She did not want to put answers into Emma Barker's mouth.

Mrs. Barker was not interested in ginseng and rattled on about something else. Cherry saw that she was not going to learn anything more about ginseng remedies here today. But there was another way she might find out! A plan took shape in her mind. It was growing late, yet not too late, not too rainy and dark—

"Mrs. Barker, this has been a delightful tea party. Now, I'm afraid I must go."

"Can't you stay and visit a little longer? Maybe Jane can join us now."

"I wish I could stay. Thank you ever so much!" Cherry was grateful to her for more than tea and cookies. Mrs. Barker had provided her with an important new lead.

Cherry said a hasty good-by to Jane, got into her car, and headed for the river road. She almost regretted what she was going to do. She'd rather not discover anything about Floyd which would distress his mother. But she wanted that old formula book.

Getting out at the old farmhouse, Cherry realized it was dangerous for her to have come here alone. She should have waited until Hal could come, too.

"Well, I'm here now. I'll be quick—and cautious."

She picked her way through patches of ginseng and of weeds, and reached the front door of the empty house. Cherry opened the door quietly, and stood there listening, looking. The house was so still she could hear the nearby river flowing. It must be swollen by the rain. This wet afternoon the sour moldy odor in the house was stronger than ever. Cherry took a deep breath of it, but was not sure whether or not it smelled like the remedy.

If someone was making the worthless remedy here, where in the house was that likely to be? Where should she look first for the ancient formula book? Or for jars of the medicine, or ginseng roots, or any telltale clue she could find? Cherry was not eager to spend any more time searching alone in this deserted place than necessary—and she preferred not to come face to face with—whom?

"If I knew the layout of the rooms—"

She peered in. Straight ahead of her was the staircase and the long, narrow hall. To her left was the empty sitting room, with only a threadbare carpet left in it. Also on her left and further down the hall was —apparently—a dining room. Although it was next to the sitting room, Cherry noticed there was no door connecting the two rooms.

The odor came from deeper inside the house.

Cherry started noiselessly down the hall. After three paces a floor board creaked. She caught her breath and halted.

"Was that someone moving around in here? Or was it my own footfall?" She listened and heard only the wind and river. "Oh, an old house is full of creaking woodwork, and on a windy, rainy day—"

She started on tiptoe again. The odor grew stronger. At the doorway of the dining room, she cautiously looked in. Along one wall—the other side of the sitting-room wall—stood a heavy, old-fashioned oak buffet. It stretched along nearly the length of the wall, standing a little askew. Except for a few worn-out dining-room chairs and the buffet, there was nothing to see.

"Maybe what I'm looking for is in the kitchen," Cherry thought. "There'd be a sink and a stove and running water, at least a pump, in the kitchen to use in making the remedy."

She hesitated. Did she hear someone in the kitchen? How warm it was in here! Had someone lighted the stove? Did she smell a kerosene stove? Well, there was only one way to find out. Go and look. But if someone *was* in there—Cherry felt the back of her neck tingle with fear.

"I won't turn back," she told herself. "I'll just take a quick look into the kitchen. I can always run for it."

The kitchen, she saw, ran across the width of the house. She was faced with a choice of whether to enter the kitchen by continuing down the hall, or by crossing through the dining room. But fading day-

light streamed through the dining-room windows—
she could be seen from the kitchen if she crossed
through. If someone was in here— Cherry decided
to stick to the shadowy hall. She crept past the dining
room, lifting and slowly setting down one foot on the
old floor boards, shifting her weight, waiting a second, then taking the next catlike step. She moved
almost soundlessly. It took her close to four minutes
to reach the kitchen.

As she came to the kitchen door, Cherry heard a
grating, scraping noise. She was so startled, she
thought her heart would fly out of her chest. She
whirled around in time to see a man's shadow running swiftly in the dining room. His shadow fell
through the dining-room doorway and across the hall
for an instant. She hesitated for a few moments, too
scared to move. Then Cherry ran back up the hall to
the dining room and peered around the doorway's
edge.

The dining room was empty. Cherry was trem-
bling. The man, whoever he was, knew that an in-
truder—she—was here. His stealth proved that. She
had to get out immediately! And by another route,
so he couldn't see and stop her. Through the kitchen?
Out the back door, and then around the far side of
the house? Yes, that should do it. She could go
through the trees and reach her car unseen.

She didn't waste any time trying to be silent.
Cherry ran through the kitchen for all she was worth.
She remembered to touch the stove as she ran. It was
stone cold. Not being used, then! Fleetingly she
thought there must be another stove in the house, but

her concern now was to escape. Thank heavens the
back door of the kitchen opened at her touch. She
fled across the big back porch, down the steps, and
around the back of the house.

She stumbled through a cluster of gnarled fruit
trees. The tangle of ginseng plants slowed her. It
seemed like an eternity until she finally reached her
car and jumped in.

Cherry started the car, pulling out of that place as
fast as she could. She took one look to see whether
anyone had followed her. No one was in sight. That
didn't mean no one was watching her! The man hid-

ing in the house could have seen who she was. He
didn't want to be seen, either—of course. She
headed the car along the weed-filled roadway and
out onto the highway, and stepped hard on the gas.
She didn't want anyone to follow her and catch up
with her.

"What an experience!" she thought. "What a narrow squeak! Not worth the risk. I didn't find a single
thing I was searching for—not the book nor ginseng
roots nor the remedy. Only a shadow."

But she knew now that someone—very likely
Floyd or some pal of his—was up to something in the

house Jane hoped to live in. The next thing was to prove his identity.

"Unless it was just a tramp, taking cover on a rainy day?" Cherry speculated. "I haven't a scrap of proof about who the man was or what he was doing. No, no, a tramp is too easy and random an explanation."

Where had the man disappeared to? He had run into the dining room, evidently from the kitchen. Once in the dining room, where had he gone to? Not back into the kitchen, or she would have seen him a few seconds later when she ran through there. Not out the dining-room windows, they were closed. Not into the hall, either, for when she saw his shadow, she was still standing in the hall. Yet when she had collected her wits and peered into the dining room, the man was gone. He had vanished, it seemed, into the wall. That certainly didn't explain anything.

CHAPTER IX

The Search

THAT EVENING CHERRY TRIED SEVERAL TIMES TO reach Dr. Hal by telephone, but he was out on emergency cases. At ten o'clock she reached him.

"Hal, I know it's late," Cherry said, "but I'd better tell you this immediately. I think someone is making that fake medicine at the abandoned farmhouse."

"Why do you think so?" Hal sounded tired, but he was not too tired to discuss this question. "Because the ginseng patch grows there?"

"That's not the only reason," Cherry said. "I went to the old house late this afternoon, and somebody was in there. . . . Yes, I went alone. Now don't scold me, Hal—" She told him about Mrs. Barker's old formula book, which was missing, and how Floyd had lied about working at the cannery. "I thought I might find Floyd or the formula book, or both, at the old farmhouse."

"Don't you go there by yourself again!" Hal said.

"Someone will have to go back there. I was so scared I left before I had a chance to search."

"Never mind that now," Hal said. "Listen, I have a lot to tell you. Is it all right if I come over this late? . . . Fine, I'll be there in five minutes."

They sat on the porch so as not to disturb Aunt Cora. The rain had stopped and the moon shone. In low voices they discussed their difficulties in finding a sample of the remedy for the Food and Drug man.

"Did he come today?" Cherry asked.

"Someone is coming tomorrow." Hal sighed. "Federal Food and Drug in Des Moines wanted to send a man who's versatile and skilled enough for this case, and that would be their resident inspector, a Mr. Collinge. But *he's* away on official business."

"Oh, no," Cherry groaned.

"Oh, yes. However," Hal said, "I was advised not to wait for him, but to get in touch with the next-nearest resident inspector. He's in Omaha, a Mr. Short. I finally was able to make contact with him at his home in Omaha this evening. And *he* promised to be in Sauk tomorrow."

"Thank goodness!" Cherry said. "Is he flying?"

"Driving. It's fastest because most direct. He has a staff car. He said he'd start tomorrow morning at six, and arrive around two in the afternoon.

"Now look, Cherry." Hal leaned forward, thinking. "I'd like to be able to tell Mr. Short where the drug is being manufactured, or distributed from, and find him a sample of it. Seems to me that you and I ought to hunt up the peddler at his shack in the woods and try to buy a jar of that concoction from him—that is, if he'd sell it to us. And maybe, for all we know, Snell or someone else is making the remedy at the shack, or distributing it from there."

"Yes, we might at least learn something at the shack," Cherry agreed. "We'd have time to go there before the Food and Drug man arrives at two."

"Where in the woods does Snell live?"

"Somewhere around Muir, I heard," Cherry said. They compared notes and found they both had patients to see tomorrow morning not far from Muir. They arranged to meet each other around ten thirty the next morning at the Muir grocery store, and fit in the visit to the peddler between their professional calls.

The rain started again the next day. As she made her rounds Cherry found the farm families worried about the heavy showers.

" 'Course, it's the twenty-first of September, so we're due for fall rains," one farmer said to her. "But my Indian corn and oats are going to be ruined if this rain don't let up."

Cherry hoped the rain would not delay the Food and Drug inspector.

A little before ten thirty Cherry drove on to the village of Muir and waited in the general store for Dr. Hal.

As she waited, she sat on a box and chatted with the storekeeper who was willing enough to talk about Old Snell.

"That old backwoods character!" the storekeeper

said. "He cuts into my business a little bit, with the wild berries and salad greens he gathers. But his main business is herbs. He says he got the folklore from his ancestors. Some folks call him a regular old-time herb doctor."

"Is he?" Cherry asked. Maybe Old Snell was the one who concocted the ginseng remedy.

"I wouldn't put any faith in a herb quack like him. I heard he concocts a brew of toadskins and cherry wine." The storekeeper made a face. "Though some folks believe he has a lot of old-fashioned know-how about herbs. Been living in the woods by himself, all these years, so they figure he's bound to've learned something."

Cherry shrugged. "How can he learn about medicine out in the woods? It takes years of study and training."

"Exactly so! It's just as well for everybody's health that Snell only peddles now and then."

"He's a recluse?"

"Yep. A real odd character."

"Do you know an acquaintance of mine, named Floyd Barker?" Cherry asked the storekeeper.

"Sure, everybody knows Floyd. He drifts all over the countryside. Haven't seen much of Floyd lately, though."

Cherry wondered why not. "Do Floyd and Old Snell ever do business together?" she asked.

"Not as far as I know of. Floyd ain't one to work."

"Well, do Floyd and Old Snell know each other?"

"Pro'bly, but I can't swear to it."

The conversation lagged. Hal arrived. He asked the storekeeper for directions to Snell's shack.

The storekeeper told them. He was curious about what the county medical officer wanted with Old Snell.

Dr. Miller did a quick, terse job of health education right there in the general store. The storekeeper listened and shook his head.

"That's awful," he said. "I've known Snell a long time, but I wouldn't shield him. I'll pass the word along, Doc."

"Good. Thanks." Cherry said thanks, too, and good-by, and went outdoors with Dr. Hal.

They decided to take Cherry's car, since it was smaller and could negotiate the woods more easily than Hal's heavier car. Cherry drove.

The rain had stopped. Still it was dim on this dirt road through the woods. They watched for the turn-off among the trees which led to where Old Snell lived. The rain had washed away any tire tracks, so they could not tell whether he or anyone else had driven through recently.

After the turnoff it was slow, bumpy going along a rough trail. The woods were silent except for birds darting over their heads. Then the peddler's shack came into view.

"Why, it's not much more than a woodshed," Cherry said.

"He's probably got it fixed up comfortably."

The shack was dark inside. They got no answer to their repeated knocking. They tried the door. Locked.

Cherry remembered having seen the peddler on that one occasion drive off in a ramshackle car, but his car was nowhere among these trees. Hal walked around the shack, looking in its closed windows.

"He's not here," Hal said. "The place is closed up and locked up. He knows we're after him, so we're wasting our time here."

"Any sign that he's making the ginseng remedy in there?" Cherry asked.

They peered in the windows. The one room was dusty and deserted. They could dimly make out a cot, kitchen chairs and table, a cookstove, a pump. Nothing more, no jars or utensils or ginseng roots.

"I still think Snell or Floyd—or whoever it is—may be making the stuff at the abandoned farmhouse," Cherry said.

"In that case let's stay out of there, at least until Mr. Short arrives," Hal said.

"Why? You think whoever's in that house may be armed?" Cherry said. She had thought of that yesterday, but had pushed the idea out of her mind.

Dr. Hal hooted at her. "What do you think? He—or they—are building up a lucrative trade out of this Nature's Herb Cure. One patient admitted to me it costs five dollars a jar. The ginseng and eggs they put into it cost them nothing, or next to nothing. Five dollars a jar! And they've been selling plenty of it around here and across the state line in Missouri. These fellows aren't going to let you and me stop their racket if they can help it."

"I can't picture that lazy, easygoing Floyd being armed," Cherry said. "If it is Floyd."

"He owns a shotgun for hunting, doesn't he?" Hal reminded her. Cherry nodded. "Probably the peddler does, too. You know, I haven't yet met this Floyd. Come on. Let's get out of these woods."

Cherry took a last look at the deserted shack. "Do you suppose the peddler's hiding out in the old farmhouse?"

"Anything is possible. Come on. Get in the car."

Hal drove back to the grocery store where he had left his car. He wanted to stop at the Barkers' and meet Floyd if possible. Or perhaps Jane would have some new information about Floyd. They still had plenty of time to spare before Mr. Short's arrival, even allowing time for their patients.

Hal said to Cherry, as he drove, "Maybe we should leave it to the Food and Drug man to search the abandoned farmhouse. He's a specially trained kind of detective—he'll know better than anyone else how to obtain evidence and how to trap this medical kind of racketeer. The more I think about it, the more I feel we should leave it to experts."

It was necessary for the Food and Drug Administration to analyze the remedy in order to determine whether it violated the Food, Drug, and Cosmetic Act.

Cherry said, "For all we know, Food and Drug might inspect the old farmhouse and not find a sample there, either."

At Muir they stopped, Hal got into his car, and Cherry followed in hers. Presently they pulled up in front of the Barkers' cottage. Floyd's jalopy was not anywhere around.

They conferred for a moment before going in. They agreed to talk with Jane privately, out in the yard. Mrs. Barker might just repeat something to Floyd, in all innocence. Even the parrot might repeat something.

Jane told them that the old peddler had not once come by the Barkers' cottage with his doubtful wares. She was puzzled about this until Cherry and Dr. Hal told her more about Old Snell. Of course the last place Snell would come would be to a friend of the doctor and nurse! Jane was relieved to hear that the Food and Drug inspector was due today. They told her this in confidence.

"If only I could get around more," Jane said, "I might try to locate a sample for you. This ankle slows me down so!"

She said she had requested an additional week's leave from her job in the East. One of her job prospects here was really shaping up. "But now this trouble about the old house—" Jane shook her head. "My mother and Bill keep writing to me, asking what's the delay about the house and farm. I can't bring myself to tell them of this ugly trouble."

And Cherry could not quite bring herself to tell Jane about her scary visit yesterday to the old farmhouse. She talked instead about Floyd, whom all three of them by now suspected. Of what, exactly? They felt he was mixed up in the medicine racket, but could not pin down their suspicions to anything tangible. Jane made a bold suggestion: confront Floyd point-blank with questions about the remedy and see how he reacted. Take him by surprise.

Cherry and Dr. Hal objected. "Floyd would simply deny that he knew anything," Hal said, "and then cover up every trace of his activities. Besides, we have no proof that it's Floyd who is behind the whole thing. We don't know who makes the drug, or where. We can't give Food and Drug even that much of a lead."

Cherry had been watching the time. It was growing close to noon. "Excuse us, now, Jane. We have to drive back to Sauk, back to work."

On the chance that the Food and Drug inspector might reach Sauk earlier than two P.M., Cherry and Dr. Hal returned to the county health office to receive him. They had plenty of medical reports to study—"although I'd rather be visiting patients," Cherry fretted, "and do the paper work some evening."

As they came in, the clerk gave Cherry a telephone message. "Would you go right over to Mrs. Grisbee's house? She called up a little while ago and said her husband is feeling sick all of a sudden. I advised her to call Dr. Clark, but she asked for you. She thinks you can give first aid, or whatever."

"I'll go right away." Cherry turned to Dr. Hal. "I won't miss seeing Mr. Short, will I?"

"Don't worry, there's time," Dr. Hal said. "Besides, he'll want to see *you.*"

Cherry left the office with her nursing bag. She walked the three blocks to the Grisbees' house. Phoebe Grisbee's huge, out-of-date car was parked in front. It always reminded Cherry of a clumsy boat or a hearse.

Phoebe Grisbee let her in and took her upstairs. She found Mr. Grisbee, in the front bedroom, nearly green in the face, sitting weakly on the bed.

"Oh-h-h, I'm sick as a billy goat!" Henry Grisbee groaned. "Sick to my stomach—throwing up—diarrhea. I don't know what's come over me!"

Cherry questioned him. What had he eaten? Had he taken any medicine?

"We-ell, I did give Henry some remedy late yesterday afternoon," Mrs. Grisbee said. She wiped his forehead. "I guess I'd better tell you the truth. Somebody talked me into giving Henry a dose—just a teeny trial dose—of that Nature's Herb Cure. I never expected it to affect him like *this!*"

"So that's what he took. After all our warnings!"

Cherry was surprised to see the fake remedy act so fast, but apparently Henry Grisbee was more susceptible to *Salmonella* bacteria than other individuals. He groaned that he'd taken only a few drops, but that was enough to upset him.

"Where did you get the Nature's Herb Cure?" Cherry asked. Phoebe Grisbee flushed and guiltily looked away. "You buy things occasionally from Old Snell," Cherry persisted. "Did you buy this concoction from him, too?"

"Well, he was here," Mrs. Grisbee admitted. "Late yesterday afternoon, after dark."

The old peddler had come out of hiding! And he was selling *in town!* This was the first time Cherry knew of that he had tackled a town with the fake remedy. He'd find many more customers concentrated in Sauk than out in open country. His presence in Sauk meant the racket was spreading to a new and larger location. Spreading! What made the old peddler so brazen?

And how could Mrs. Grisbee, who knew better, have been so foolish as to buy and use the dangerous stuff? Cherry asked her that. Mrs. Grisbee said defensively:

"Old Snell asked me not to be prejudiced, just to try it. He's sold me other things that've done me good. I'm an old customer, and he saw that Mr. Grisbee was feeling poorly, so he gave him one little dose free. Just to try it."

"As a favor to you," Cherry said dryly.

"Well, *he* did *me* a favor. He left his usual route and came into Sauk especially to bring me some things I wanted." Cherry did not believe the peddler's altruistic tale. "As long as he made a trip especially for me," Mrs. Grisbee went on, "I felt I ought to buy something extra, or at least do something for him. So when he asked me just to let Henry try this Nature's Herb Cure, I did."

Mr. Grisbee muttered, "Some favor to me!"

Cherry shook her head. She set about taking his temperature, pulse, and respiration, and making the man as comfortable as possible. "We'd better call Dr. Clark," Cherry said. Mrs. Grisbee nodded, and went downstairs to telephone the doctor.

"Honestly," Cherry said, when Mrs. Grisbee came upstairs again, "I'm surprised at you, letting Mr. Grisbee swallow such junk. You know better."

Mr. Grisbee groaned in agreement. Phoebe Grisbee said:

"I—I thought the herbs in it made it all right. Snell was positive it would do Henry heaps of good. In fact, he was so certain that I'd want to buy a jar of it, he promised to wait for me at his shack in the woods tomorrow."

"He did!" What a piece of good luck! Why, that would give the Food and Drug man a chance to nab the peddler!

"He'll be at the shack late tomorrow afternoon," Mrs. Grisbee added.

"Why tomorrow?" Cherry asked. She checked herself from saying that until now the old peddler had apparently been hiding out, that this morning his shack had been closed up. "Why tomorrow especially?"

"Oh, Snell told me he's been staying and visiting with an old crony," Mrs. Grisbee said, "but tomorrow he's moving back to his own place."

Cherry was puzzled about the sudden boldness of the old peddler. Why did he choose this particular time to come out of hiding? Why was he beginning to sell the remedy in the towns *now*?

Phoebe Grisbee rattled on, trying to excuse herself. "Old Snell had a long list of word-of-mouth testimonials, from people I actually know here and across the river, so I thought—"

"He's selling across the river in Missouri, too? At present?"

"Land's sakes, yes! Said he has lots of new customers in Missouri."

Cherry stared at her. "Mrs. Grisbee, you're entirely too trusting. Just because Snell is an old acquaintance! By the way, have you any Nature's Herb Cure left?"

"No. I never had any in the first place. Old Snell gave me a bit—a teaspoonful. Henry wouldn't take but a taste. Why?"

"I'll tell you later."

Cherry prepared the patient for the doctor's visit. Within a few minutes Dr. Aloysius Clark arrived. He examined and questioned Mr. Grisbee.

"It looks to me," Dr. Clark said, "as if you're more miserable than sick."

It was a good thing, Dr. Clark remarked to Cherry, that Mr. Grisbee had taken very little of the fake remedy.

As soon as the doctor no longer needed her, Cherry hurried back to the county health office.

CHAPTER X

A Ruse Is Set Up

IF CHERRY HAD NOT BEEN EXPECTING THE FOOD AND
Drug inspector, she would not have recognized the
man talking with Dr. Hal as a special kind of detective. This quiet, studious-looking man seemed
more like a scientist or a teacher.

"Here she is," Dr. Hal said, as Cherry came in,
and both men rose. "Mr. Short, this is our county
nurse, Cherry Ames. Cherry, the United States Food
and Drug inspector—"

"I'm Paul Short," he said, and held out his hand to
her. "Dr. Miller tells me that people here are taking
this dangerous remedy in spite of a warning." He
spoke in a quiet, thoughtful way. "We'd better move
quickly."

The three of them sat down around the desk.
Cherry was bursting with the news that the peddler
would be back at his shack late tomorrow afternoon,

but she of course waited to hear how the Food and Drug man would proceed.

"The first thing I want to know," Mr. Short said, "is who manufactures this Nature's Herb Cure?"

"We don't know, sir," Dr. Hal said. "We have a suspicion that it may be made at an abandoned farmhouse near here, but that's only a suspicion. All we know for certain is that an old peddler named Snell sells it secretly."

Hal handed the inspector the jar which Mrs. Swaybill had given Cherry. He explained that the manufacturer's address on the label was a false one.

Mr. Short read the label and shood his head. "The usual hokum. Crude directions for use, and the claims are fantastic. This is grounds for Food and Drug action."

Cherry asked, "Is this what you call misbranding?"

"The worst kind," Mr. Short said. "We could put someone in jail for this—if we could get an official sample."

He explained that an official sample was one which the Food and Drug inspector collects and seals, with a printed form on the seal which he fills out and signs. Although Mr. Short was most interested to see the jar which the county doctor and nurse had obtained, he had to obtain the official sample himself. Without it, the Food and Drug Administration could take no action.

"Before we discuss that," Mr. Short said, "you must tell me all you know about this remedy, particularly how it is being sold and falsely promoted. I realize," the Food and Drug inspector added, "it's not possible for you two to furnish me with complete evidence. That's what I'm here for. Any leads you can give me—"

Dr. Hal and Cherry told him what facts they knew. The inspector listened closely.

"The Food and Drug Administration needs evidence. Proof," he said. "We can accept your testimony, as competent medical persons, until we get our own sample and make our own analysis of the remedy. We absolutely must get an official sample. And what we need is *proof* that the peddler is selling the stuff out of state."

Hal scowled, and Cherry guessed he was trying to think how to proceed with the search.

"Have you any ideas about where I'll be able to get an official sample?" Paul Short asked. "Our usual procedure is to go to the place of manufacture and inspect the premises, and take a sample. But we can't do that since you're not sure where this stuff is being made. Of course I could go have a look in the abandoned farmhouse, on a chance—"

Cherry said, "If you'd like to try to get a sample from the peddler, he'll be waiting at his shack in the woods late tomorrow afternoon."

"He will!" Dr. Hal exclaimed, and Mr. Short's eyes gleamed with interest. Hal demanded, "How come Snell will be there? How did you find out about it?"

Cherry described her visit with Phoebe Grisbee.

Paul Short gave Cherry an appraising look. "I have an idea what to do about that appointment, if it's acceptable to Miss Ames. If you can persuade your friend, Mrs. Grisbee, to go to the peddler's shack—"

"Why, I'll—I'll certainly ask Mrs. Grisbee to go and buy a jar of Nature's Herb Cure from the peddler for us. And I'll do anything further I can to help."

"Anything? Do you mean that? If you'd be willing to take a risk, Miss Ames, I think we could move in on this case tomorrow afternoon. At the shack. But I warn you, it's risky. I'm not urging you. It'll be perfectly all right if you say no."

"Say no to what?" Hal asked.

The inspector took a long breath. "This is the plan I have in mind. I want Cherry Ames to go with Mrs. Grisbee to the peddler's shack. I want her to pose as a patient. Pose as Mrs. Grisbee's niece from another state, who's been taken sick here. Buy some of the remedy from the peddler on his claim that it will cure you. And buy it with the peddler's knowing that you plan to take it home with you to another state." The inspector leaned toward them. "Do you see? That will give us the official sample, and will constitute proof of secret deliveries to out-of-state customers."

"But—but the peddler knows who I am," Cherry said. "He'd recognize me."

"That's exactly where the risk comes in," Mr. Short said. "You'd have to disguise yourself a little, and pretend to be sick."

"Cherry?" Hal asked. "Think you want to take such a risk? Snell is obviously an eccentric and may be dangerous. He might even be armed."

She was trying to think. She was aware of the

124

danger, but that was not the main thing. She thought angrily of the hurt done to so many of her patients. She must not let Snell slip away.

"You and Mrs. Grisbee wouldn't go alone," the Food and Drug inspector said. "I'd go with you, and whoever the local police could send—your sheriff or his deputy—someone to give you protection, someone who can make an arrest on my complaint."

"I'd go along, too," Hal said to Cherry. "*If* you go."

The plan began to catch fire in her imagination. She thought of Phoebe Grisbee's huge old sedan. It had plenty of room in the back seat for three men to sit on the floor, unseen. With three men along—

"I'll do it," said Cherry.

"Are you sure?" Mr. Short asked her. She nodded. "That's wonderful! That will be invaluable help."

He coached her in detail as to what she and Phoebe Grisbee were to say and do. As for himself, he and the sheriff would have to get a warrant of arrest from the nearest federal court.

"The nearest is in Des Moines," Hal said.

The Food and Drug inspector looked at his wrist watch. "It's twenty to three now. The court closes at four, and opens again at ten in the morning. Let's see. It took me approximately three and three-quarters hours today to drive the hundred and fifty or more miles from Des Moines to Sauk. That means seven and a half hours for the round trip. Figure about half an hour to get the warrant, and a little time to get meals and gas—" He broke off to ask, "Has Sauk got an airport? Or anyone with a private plane who'll fly the sheriff and me to Des Moines?"

"Unfortunately no," Hal said.

"Well, then," Mr. Short said, "the sheriff and I had better start pretty soon for Des Moines, stay there overnight, get the warrant at ten, and drive back here tomorrow. I don't want to risk being late for that appointment with Snell."

As important as it was to find and inspect the place where the drug was manufactured, Mr. Short decided that the chance to nab the peddler and obtain an official sample was still more urgent. The question of the place of manufacture could wait for a few hours longer.

Now that their plan of action was decided on, they talked for a few minutes about how Mr. Short worked. In order to do his job, he was highly trained in the organic sciences and in his particular kind of scientific crime-detection techniques.

"Sounds exciting," Dr. Hal said.

"Sometimes collecting samples is a little risky," Paul Short said. "You'll find out tomorrow afternoon. Incidentally, I wish you'd both still be alert for a sample, in case our ruse falls through. Though I think Snell will show up."

"Next thing," said Cherry, "is to persuade Mrs. Grisbee to go along with our plan."

While Dr. Hal and Mr. Short went to another part of the courthouse building to see the sheriff, Cherry went to Phoebe Grisbee's house.

Thank goodness Henry Grisbee was asleep. Phoebe was surprised to see Cherry again so soon, even more surprised when Cherry asked her for a pledge of secrecy.

"I'll be quiet as the grave. Can't I even tell your aunt or my husband about what we're going to do?"

"Not yet," Cherry said. "Snell is breaking the law and making lots of people sick. Your husband, for instance. Snell is wanted by the federal government."

Phoebe Grisbee's eyes and mouth opened. "Snell? A—a criminal? I thought he was just a poor lonely old backwoods fellow—"

She listened solemnly while Cherry told her the chief facts of the racket, and then outlined the Food and Drug man's strategy for tomorrow afternoon.

"Will you co-operate, Mrs. Grisbee? Will you take this risk in order to help yourself and your neighbors?"

"Well, I do lots of community work—I guess tomorrow afternoon would be for the general welfare, too, wouldn't it?" Phoebe Grisbee's round face was very sober as she thought it over. "I could ask a neighbor to stay with my husband. All right, I'll go. Though I don't know what Mr. Grisbee will say when he finds out."

"Good for you!" Cherry squeezed her plump hand. "I'll come back here tomorrow around four."

"I'll have some clothes ready for you to wear as a disguise," Phoebe Grisbee said. "Mercy! We'll both of us have to do a good piece of play acting."

From Mrs. Grisbee's house, Cherry notified Dr. Hal that her aunt's friend would take part in the plan. Mr. Short and the sheriff had already left for Des Moines. Then Cherry drove out into the country to see her nursing cases.

It would be just today, when she was preoccupied, that a rural storekeeper told her of a new family with a crippled child. Rumor said that the little boy had had polio a year ago; he wore a brace and limped. The family had just moved into the county, and the other children wondered why he did not come to school.

Cherry drove to where the road ended, then got out of her car and walked. She found, on an under-developed farm, a brave family and a seriously handicapped boy of seven. There was no possibility of his traveling to school. A teacher would have to come to him. Or, Cherry realized, the doctors might decide eventually to send Billy to a crippled children's hospital, or to the University Hospital for surgery, where his deformity might be corrected. She told the family of the good work done by the State Services for Crippled Children, a team of specialists who came from the University of Iowa Hospital to hold clinics in various parts of the state. It was the county nurse's job to find patients and prepare them for the team's visit, under direction of the local physicians.

"Can they help our Billy?" the family asked.

Cherry gave Billy and his family all the encouragement she honestly could. She wanted very much to see this little boy walk normally, and run, and some-day play baseball with other boys his age. She was so glad she'd found him.

Cherry visited a few other cases. Her last call of the afternoon was at a country boardinghouse, to advise the pleasant woman who owned it on a minor health problem. This section of the county was not familiar to Cherry; she had made only one call around here, much earlier, with her nursing supervisor, Miss Hudson. The roads were still muddy from the rains. Cherry consulted her map to locate the paved highways back to Sauk.

She drove past woods and river, thinking about her patients, and did not notice a parked or stalled car until she was nearly on top of it. Two men were standing in the muddy road beside the car. They hailed her, and Cherry stopped.

"Hey, miss! Do us a favor?" one man said to her. His manner was almost insolent.

Cherry looked quizzically at him and the other burly man. They had hard faces, hard eyes. They wore flashy, expensive sports clothes, brand new. It was obvious that they were city men dressed as sportsmen. Cherry glanced at the license plate on their shiny car, and recognized it as a St. Louis plate.

"Excuse me, miss—" The second man made a clumsy effort to act polite. "Excuse me, miss. If it wouldn't be too much trouble to help us out—"

For an instant Cherry thought they wanted her to minister first aid here at the roadside. But they gave no sign of recognizing her as the county nurse.

"We got stuck in the mud, see?" the second man continued. "So if you'd stop off at the nearest filling station and tell the guy there to come over with his tow truck— Say, tell him we'll pay him plenty, so he should hurry up."

"All right, I'll tell him," Cherry said. She waited for them to say thanks. They did not. The pause grew into an embarrassment among them. The first man said uneasily:

"Tell him to hurry up, because we're going fishing, see? Uh—we're having ourselves a little vacation around here. Staying at Mrs. Moody's boarding-house, getting in a little fishing."

"Oh, yes," said Cherry. She did not believe that they were going to fish. They evidently had some other business around here. Their sports clothes were like a ludicrous disguise.

"I'll tell the man at the filling station," Cherry said, and she drove off. Whew! She wanted to get away from the two strangers as fast as possible.

The road followed along the river about a mile to the filling station. Cherry turned in there. The place was spick-and-span, the sign said it belonged to George Huntley. He was a brisk, cheerful young man who wiped off Cherry's windshield for her while she gave him the strangers' message.

"I know the two you mean," the young man said. "Sure, I'll haul them out of the mud."

"Who are those men?" Cherry asked.

"I don't know. Beats me what they're doing around these parts. I never saw them before. Neither did Mrs. Moody, their landlady." George Huntley finished with the windshield. He said thoughtfully, "They *say* they're fishing. I hear they're gone all hours of the day—*and* night—but how come they haven't brought home any catch?"

Cherry admitted, "I don't much like their looks."

"Neither do I, miss. Neither do any of us. In fact,

folks around here think those two are suspicious-looking characters. Criminals, gangsters, for all we know. Mrs. Moody'd like to get them out of her boardinghouse, but she's afraid to start any trouble with them."

"How long have they been here?" Cherry asked.

"Came here Monday. Late Monday. Wait—I said no one around here knows those two men, but I was mistaken. Now mind you, this is only hearsay, and *he* denies it, but— Gosh, maybe I shouldn't repeat things like this."

"I'm the county nurse, Mr. Huntley," said Cherry. She showed him her credentials with her name. "I take an interest in everything that goes on in this county. Please tell me whatever news you have."

"Well," the young man said reluctantly, "don't repeat it, but a farmer near here said he saw a fellow named Floyd Barker with those two men. They all were close to the river, on this farmer's land, sort of hiding in the trees and talking. When the farmer rode close by on his tractor, they all ran off like turkeys. Guess they had their car nearby, or Floyd had his jalopy, because one, two, three—they were gone!"

"So Floyd Barker knows those two men," Cherry said. She felt a little sick.

"You know Floyd?" the young man asked Cherry. She nodded. "Well, Miss Ames, maybe I'm saying something untrue about a friend of yours. I only have this farmer's word for the whole thing. Some of us happened to bump into Floyd yesterday, and we jollied him about what's *he* doing with those two characters? Why, Floyd denied up and down that he knows those two men. Swore he's never even seen them. So maybe the farmer is mistaken and Floyd's telling the truth."

"Maybe," Cherry said, trying to conceal her doubt. "Maybe."

She asked George Huntley whether he knew anything about Nature's Herb Cure, or had seen Old Snell around here. He had not. Apparently the peddler—the only man selling the stuff—had not reached this area yet. Cherry thanked the young man at the filling station and drove away.

She thought about the two strangers as she drove home toward Sauk. Their presence here meant that the racket was not as local and limited as she and Hal had assumed—not if the two St. Louis men were here to talk to Floyd. For that, evidently, was the real reason for their visit: to talk with Floyd. Was it about the ginseng-remedy racket?

George Huntley had said the two men arrived late Monday. Cherry thought back over recent events.

On Saturday the ginseng roots had been stolen from her car. On Monday she and Hal had learned the results of the laboratory investigations, and had issued their first warnings. So! . . .

Could the two men possibly have other business with Floyd? If so, why did they have to confer at a secret place at the river's edge?

It was a long drive across the county. The river road led her past the abandoned farm. Cherry looked sharply for any sign of life in the house or around the grounds. She saw no one, no lights in the house, although it was dusk. But that was as usual.

She headed for home. She felt discouraged. With the two hard-faced men here, working with Floyd to promote the remedy, the job of the Food and Drug inspector could be harder and more dangerous. Undoubtedly the two men were working with the peddler, too.

It dawned on Cherry why Old Snell suddenly was brazenly selling the remedy in the towns, why he was boldly returning to his shack—now that the two St. Louis men were here! Why, those men must be backing Snell up with money, even with a promise of gangster force.

Cherry wondered whether Snell would be alone tomorrow at the shack, or whether Floyd or the two men might be with him. Sooner or later Mr. Short would have to encounter Floyd and possibly the two St. Louis men. She only hoped that she and Hal could be of some help. She arrived at Aunt Cora's feeling very tired.

"My, what a long face, Cherry," her aunt said. "You look as if this has been a hard day for you."

"It's been an exciting day, Aunt Cora."

She wished that she could tell her aunt about the entire situation, about the Food and Drug man's plan, about the suspicions centering around Floyd and the old farmhouse. She had not confided in her aunt, nor in anyone but Jane; this was on Dr. Hal's advice. He felt that if talk spread, it might reach the makers and distributors of the fake medicine. Once alerted, they could flee, and escape prosecution. Of course Aunt Cora, like everyone else for miles around, had heard of Nature's Herb Cure, and the medical warning against it. That much Cherry could talk with her about. Even so, Cherry decided she did not want to talk or even think about that upsetting problem for a few hours.

"It *has* been a hard day, Aunt Cora," Cherry said. "If it won't keep you waiting too long for supper, I'd like to take a warm bath."

"It won't keep me waiting at all," Aunt Cora said. "I'll tell you what. Let's take the evening off. Let's go out for supper, and go to a movie, or go visiting. You think about what you'd like to do while you're taking your bath."

Cherry smiled at her aunt. "You've put me in a better humor already. Thanks!" She went upstairs, with her aunt calling after her not to hurry.

Cherry soaked herself in the bathtub, not thinking about a thing. As she relaxed, a fresh idea came to her.

"The cave! Why didn't I think of that before!"

CHAPTER XI

~~~~~~~~~~~~~~~~~~~~~~~~~~~~~~~~~~~~

Discoveries

"THE CAVE—WHY DIDN'T I EVER REALIZE BEFORE that the cave is close to the abandoned farmhouse?" Cherry asked herself. "That cave was blockaded. Suppose the blockade has some purpose? Is there any connection between the cave and whatever is going on in the old house?"

Cherry dressed quickly and ran downstairs to ask Aunt Cora whether she knew, or had heard, any tales about the cave.

"I did once hear that some caves or hiding places around here have a long history," Aunt Cora said. Cherry recalled Jane's saying that the old farmhouse was reported to hold a secret—a secret over a hundred years old.

"Is there anyone around Sauk who would remember? Anyone interested in local history?" Cherry asked.

"Yes. Phoebe Grisbee's old uncle. He's a scholarly old man, and his forebears were among the first settlers in Iowa. But he's so old and frail, I don't know whether he receives many visitors."

"It's important," Cherry said. "Please don't ask me any questions."

"Well, really! I must say—" Then Aunt Cora smiled. "No, I won't say. I'll go phone Mr. Marquette and ask if we may pay him a call."

After a telephone conversation, Aunt Cora returned to say that the old man would see them this evening, if they could conveniently come right away.

"We mustn't keep him up too late," Aunt Cora said. "Let's skip supper until later, shall we?"

In an old house at the end of town, Cherry and her aunt found a more vigorous old man than they had expected to see. He was, in fact, delighted to have company. Cherry thought she saw traces of Indian as well as French descent in his long, narrow, hawk-nosed face, fine black eyes, and lean figure.

"Yes, ladies, there are indeed some woods and houses with a history in this part of Iowa," Louis Marquette said. "That's because of our Des Moines River, and our proximity to the Mississippi River. The two rivers meet near here, as you know."

Cherry asked what specific history a century-old farmhouse, or a cave near it and near the river, might have.

"A century ago. Or longer, you say." The old man thought for a moment. "That would take us back to the days just before the Civil War. In those days, or

rather, nights, runaway slaves from southern planta-
tions secretly followed the Mississippi to escape to
the North and freedom—"

He began to tell them stories of the Underground
Railway. There never was an actual railroad; he explained that was a code name for escape routes, on
foot. "Stations" were hiding places along the way for
runaway Negroes. "Conductors" were sympathetic
Northerners who opposed slavery and helped smuggle the fugitives northward to free Canada. Slave
hunters, men on horseback armed with whips and
guns and bloodhounds, scoured the North, demand-
ing that the slaves be returned. The law of the land,
the Fugitive Slave Act, was on the slave hunters' side,
and big rewards were offered for the runaways.

"Anyone who undertook to hide a fugitive or two
or three, and pass them safely further northward,"
Mr. Marquette said, "had to find, or build, safe hiding places. That's why you still can find houses and
barns with secret rooms, and concealed routes of
various kinds. Now, I've heard of a cave near here
located at the river's edge, at a narrow point in the
Des Moines River—"

Cherry felt the back of her neck tingle with excitement. The cave in Riverside Park was near the Des
Moines River. And the river narrowed there! At the
picnic the Sunday before Labor Day, some of the
boys had easily swum over to the Missouri shore and
back.

"—where it was easier, being narrower," the old
man was saying, "for the runaways to cross by skiff.
They crossed the river by night, from the slave

state of Missouri to the free state of Iowa. When they reached this side, a 'conductor' hid them somewhere and kept them for a few days, or overnight, until the next 'conductor' farther north signaled that it was safe to smuggle them along to his station." Old Mr. Marquette paused. "We had only a few conductors and stations around here. Rare, here. Most of the escaping slaves, after following the Mississippi northward, turned east rather than west and followed along the Ohio River. But we had a few 'stations.'"

"About the cave, Mr. Marquette," Cherry said. She noticed her aunt observing her excitement. "Where is that cave, please? And you said some houses had a secret room—where is there such a house around here?"

Both the old man and her aunt smiled.

"I'd gladly tell you if I knew," Mr. Marquette said. "In a hundred years people forget a secret. Mind you, only a handful of persons ever knew such secrets in the first place. Houses get torn down. Old trails are overgrown, or paved over now."

"But a cave!" Aunt Cora said. "A cave remains."

Mr. Marquette shook his head and said the only hiding places he'd known about no longer existed.

Cherry was disappointed—but excited at learning this much. Houses with secret rooms! Cherry recalled how she had seen the shadow of a man's figure in the old farmhouse and how it had vanished, seemingly into the wall. Could there be a hidden room in the old farmhouse?

And the blockaded cave! The cave had seemed to hold a passageway, blocked by a pile of dirt. *Was* there a passageway or secret route? Did it, by any chance, lead from the cave to the nearby old farmhouse? If so, to where in the farmhouse?

Cherry wanted to go first thing tomorrow to the old farm and explore. But with the two strangers from St. Louis in the vicinity, would that be too dangerous? She asked her aunt to wait a few minutes on Dr. Clark's porch while she stopped by to tell Dr. Hal what she had learned.

"I'm not sure you've really learned anything," Hal said kindly. "Don't get your hopes up too high. Local lore might be factual, or it might not."

"If I could ever get mad at you, Hal Miller, it would be now!" Cherry said.

"Well, I notice your old Mr. Marquette couldn't show you a map, or name names or locations," Hal said.

"Hmm. Still—listening to him talk makes the old hiding places awfully real. Hal, do you suppose there's a secret route near that farm?"

"Cherry! All you have is a hypothesis."

"My dear Mr. Scientist, do you suppose Floyd and the others are making some special use of the house and cave for their Nature's Herb Cure racket?"

"It's possible. I'll tell you this," Hal said, "I'd rather not enter the cave or farmhouse again if we can avoid it."

"S-sh!" Cherry said. "Aunt Cora is outside on the porch, and I don't want her to hear and worry."

Cherry and Hal exchanged good nights, and Cherry went out to her aunt.

"You're so patient to wait for me," Cherry said.

"You must be half starved by now. I know I am."

"Well, yes," Aunt Cora confessed. "Let's go to Smith's Restaurant. It's never too late to go there."

It was growing close to ten P.M., which in a little farming town like Sauk was very late indeed. Most people were in bed by now, because they rose at sunup. The few blocks to the town's only restaurant were dark and deserted.

The lunch counter at the front of Smith's was serving all-night truck drivers. Cherry and her aunt went on into the back dining room, where they sat down in one of the booths. It seemed empty here, as usual.

The waitress came and they gave their order. At first Cherry thought she and Aunt Cora were the only patrons. Then she heard a low murmur of men's voices. She looked over her shoulder and saw them. Floyd Barker and the two hard-looking strangers were sitting almost out of sight in the farthest booth. They had their heads together, talking in low, urgent voices.

"Aunt Cora," Cherry whispered, "don't call me by name in here." She slid into the corner of the booth. "Please! Let's keep quiet."

Aunt Cora was astonished, but co-operated. Cherry did not want Floyd and the two St. Louis men to see her—to see that she had observed them together, to realize that now she would link the three of them in her fight against the fake drug. That would force them into stronger, more devious tactics.

Cherry half rose, to go, to hurry out. Or was it safer to sit tight and be inconspicuous?

The waitress came with the first of their food. That settled it. If she and Aunt Cora walked out leaving their food untouched, and the waitress asked questions, *that* would be noticeable.

Cherry, somehow, got through a miserable meal. Floyd and the two strangers left first. They walked rapidly through the room looking straight ahead, not talking. Had they seen her? Cherry thought they had. She heard a car start out in the street.

"Now can you tell me what's wrong?" Aunt Cora asked. She looked terribly worried.

Cherry slowly shook her head. "I'm sorry, Aunt Cora. Not yet. Soon, though—"

That Wednesday night Cherry's dreams were troubled. She woke up far too early, impatient for a decent hour to telephone Dr. Hal. She told him about the incident in Smith's Restaurant.

He was as alarmed as she was. "I'll tell Mr. Short and the sheriff," he said. "I'll probably see them before you do, today."

"Yes, I'm going right out on nursing calls this morning," Cherry said.

"I'd better tell them, too, about those stories of caves and hiding places that you heard last evening from old Mr. Marquette," Hal said. "No, on second thought, I won't. They're vague, and anyway, Mr. Steeley is bound to know all the local hearsay."

There was a pause in their conversation. In the face of last night's ugly development, neither of them knew what to say.

"Well, Cherry," Hal said, "keep your eyes open

on your visits for a sample—just in case Snell tricks us this afternoon."

"I will. See you late this afternoon. I wish us luck." Cherry hung up, conscious of her aunt trying not to overhear, but worried all the same.

Cherry paid quick visits to six trustworthy former patients. Every one of them, acting on her and Dr. Hal's earlier instructions, had thrown away Nature's Herb Cure. No sample there for Mr. Short to collect. Nor had these persons seen the old peddler. They thought he must have changed his route.

At noon Dr. Hal notified Cherry at her office that he had driven across the river to Missouri that morning, and talked with the Swaybills' cousins. Neither they nor their neighbors had kept any of the fake remedy. They had not seen the old peddler, either. No other peddler sold the stuff.

Cherry heard something interesting from one of the other doctors in the county when she called him to report on one of his patients. Dr. Boudineau, who traveled all over the county, said he had not observed ginseng growing anywhere except on the abandoned farm. And he told her that the peddler had been seen in Red Oaks two or three days ago. It was a small town in an area where, so far, Cherry had no patients. Old Snell had tried to persuade a druggist there to stock and sell Nature's Herb Cure, and had offered profitable terms. The druggist would have nothing to do with the plan.

So the peddler was trying to expand the racket in several new places! He was changing locations in order to evade her and Hal's public warnings!

Unfortunately, her afternoon's schedule took her not to individual patients who might have a sample of the stuff, but to one of the county's rural high schools, in a far corner of the county. Dr. Rand, one of the county's physicians, had asked her to assist in giving inoculations against typhoid.

Cherry assisted with the immunization clinic at the rural high school. Her work took up most of the early afternoon. Afterward, she spent a few more precious minutes talking to the teen-age boys and girls.

Many of them belonged to the 4-H Club, sponsored by the United States Department of Agriculture, and told Cherry they hoped to win awards at the fair. The boys were growing fine bulls, hogs, colts, and were raising prize corn and vegetables, here in the richest soil in the nation. The girls grew flowers of all kinds, did fine baking, breadmaking, canning, and preserving, and sewed everything from clothing to curtains and quilts.

The girls asked Cherry whether she would head a 4-H Club project for them in health, nursing, and first aid. A good many of the boys wanted to take part in that, too. Cherry was happy to say yes. She left it to them to decide, and notify her, when and where they would hold their meetings. It was all she could do to break away from these friendly boys and girls.

Cherry left the school building and started back toward Sauk. On the way she stopped at a highway telephone booth and called Jane Fraser. Both Hal and Mr. Short wanted to learn from Jane where Floyd was today.

"Between this party line and that talkative parrot, I'll have to choose my words carefully," Cherry thought. She listened to the operator ringing the Barkers' number and hoped Floyd would not answer.

Jane's voice came on. In a kind of double talk, Cherry conveyed her question. All Jane was able to reply guardedly was: "I don't know for certain. I think our friend went rabbit hunting."

Rabbit hunting in the woods? Near Snell's shack? Cherry said, "I'll be in touch with you soon again. Right now I have an appointment with a patient." She wished she could tell Jane that the "patient" was herself.

CHAPTER XII

The Old Peddler Reappears

PHOEBE GRISBEE WAS AS GOOD AS HER WORD. SHE had ready several coats and scarfs for Cherry to choose from, and a box of pale face powder to tone down her rosy cheeks. Working together, they managed to make Cherry resemble a wan country cousin. Cherry hid her dark hair under a scarf and added a pair of dark glasses. Even so, she wasn't sure the peddler would not recognize her as the county nurse.

"Talk in a high-pitched voice," Phoebe Grisbee advised. "Drawl, like the Missourians do."

Cherry tried it and thought she wouldn't fool a soul. She'd better say very little. She still didn't look sick; she made herself slump and droop.

"You look almost as miserable as Henry feels." Phoebe Grisbee chuckled. "A joke on us, pretending you're the patient. Hope I drive all right, excited as I am."

They went out to the Grisbees' garage. Getting

into the car, Cherry discovered that Dr. Hal, Mr. Short, and Mr. Steeley, the sheriff, were already on the floor in the back of the car. They must have slipped in under cover of gathering dusk. Hal grinned at her; he was so tall he had to crouch. Sheriff Steeley carried a revolver in a holster. Cherry saw the bump it made under his jacket.

"All right," said the sheriff, "let's be on our way. We have the warrant of arrest. Ladies, stay in the car while you talk to the peddler. *Don't* go into the shack. If there's a fight, get down on the car seat or floor. Is that understood, ladies?"

They said yes. Paul Short had instructed Cherry yesterday what she must say to the peddler.

Mrs. Grisbee backed the car out of the garage and drove out of Sauk along a back street. Sweat stood out on her round face by the time she drove within sight of the woods. No one in the car spoke. The palms of Cherry's hands grew clammy. She watched but saw no other cars.

They entered the woods. Mrs. Grisbee evidently had come to the peddler's shack before, for she knew the trail to follow. They passed Snell's ramshackle car, parked in a clearing. When the shack hove into view, Cherry saw that this time it had a light in it.

"Park as close to the shack as you can," Mr. Steeley muttered from the back of the car. "Leave your headlights off."

Cherry was glad of that, and of the half-dark of the forest; the hazy dimness aided her disguise. Mrs. Grisbee parked the car and called out:

"Oh, Snell! Sne-ell! It's Mrs. Grisbee."

They waited. Was the peddler suspicious of the girl with her? Cherry heard Phoebe's heavy breathing. The door of the shack creaked. Old Snell came toward them.

For the first time Cherry had a close look at him. He was like a figure out of an old folk tale, or out of a disturbing dream—odd, uncouth, like no one she had ever seen before. It was no wonder some people credited him with almost magical powers. Except, Cherry thought, that his strangeness was part of a carefully calculated act.

"Hi, Mis' Grisbee," he said in a cracked voice. "How's yer husband today? Feelin' better after that herb cure I gave ye?"

"Yes, thanks, Snell, he's better," Phoebe Grisbee lied. "Your medicine is good stuff."

"I told ye 't'was. I know a thing or two about herbs and nat'ral cures. Who's that ye got with ye?"

"My cousin, Hettie Grisbee. She's from Missouri—Leaderville—on the other side of the river. She came over today to visit me."

Cherry nodded to the peddler, not trusting herself to speak yet. He said "Howdy" and stared at her.

"I guess our Iowa air don't agree with Hettie," Mrs. Grisbee said. "She's feeling poorly today."

The old peddler walked closer to the car, so close to Cherry that she could have reached out and touched his faded garments.

"Got a headache?" he croaked at Cherry. "Stomach bother ye?"

She nodded and said in a high, thin voice, "I feel hot and cold all over and dizzy."

"Hah! Then I know what's the matter with ye and what'll cure ye. If ye don't object to some old-time doctorin'?" he asked sharply.

"We-ell—" Cherry pretended to hesitate, as the Food and Drug man had coached her. "Cousin Phoebe thinks you can help me."

"Yes, that's right!" Mrs. Grisbee picked up the cue. Her voice was too loud. It rang out in these lonely woods. "I told Hettie I was coming over here to get some more of that Nature's Herb Cure for myself, and maybe it'd help her, too. I thought maybe we'd each buy a jar from you."

"I—I don't like to dose myself with a lot of medicines," Cherry said for the peddler's benefit. She tried to drawl, like a Missourian. "When I go back home to Leaderville tonight, I'll just sleep off this sick feeling."

The peddler was not one to miss out on a sale. "Now looky here, Miss Hettie," he said. "Why'n't you listen to Mis' Grisbee and me? I ain't a quack. Why go on sufferin' all the way back to Leaderville and all night—when my Nature's Herb Cure'll fix you up in a jiffy?"

"It's good, Hettie." Mrs. Grisbee pretended to urge her. "I can testify to that."

"Sure it's good," Old Snell said. "There ain't hardly an ache or fever or sickness that this here medicine won't help. That's because," he explained, "only the purest, strongest, nat'ral herbs are in the makin's. I don't claim it'll cure ye if ye're half dead already with lung trouble or somethin' dire. No, ma'am, I wouldn't be honest with ye if I claimed that. But go ask Mis' Grisbee's neighbors, and they'll tell you by the dozens that it got them over a lot of sickness. Without foolin' around with a doctor and all his newfangled ideas and a big fat bill, neither. These here herbs cured my parents and my grandparents before them, and what *they* taught me'll cure you, too, Miss Hettie."

The peddler spoke with such conviction that Cherry wondered whether he half believed in his spiel. At least she had obtained the seller's statement of false claims, which the Food and Drug inspector needed.

Mrs. Grisbee said loudly, "Snell makes it himself. Don't you, Snell?"

He said "Mmm" vaguely. Cherry knew that the Food and Drug inspector, listening from the floor of the car, could not count that as a statement. She leaned back as if a wave of nausea came over her.

"Look at the poor girl!" Mrs. Grisbee exclaimed. The peddler did look. Cherry held her breath as he peered at her with the shrewd, heartless eyes of a fox. "Look at how sick she is!" Mrs. Grisbee said. "We'd better stop talking and buy some medicine."

"Come on into the shack if ye feel sick," the peddler invited her.

And face the light in the shack! Cherry shook her head and drew the scarf closer around her face. The peddler was watching her.

"How much is the medicine?" Cherry asked, to distract him. "If it's as good as you both say, maybe I'll take two jars back to Leaderville with me." She said this to establish the interstate commerce part of the sale.

"Ye can do that. It's five dollars a jar, nine-fifty for the two jars," the peddler said, "and a wild bargain considerin' what a doctor'd charge. If ye want some more next week or so, Miss Hettie, I'll fetch it to ye next time I drive across the river. Just let Mis' Grisbee know ye'll expect me. Uh—I'd appreciate it if ye'd keep mum about this, because the confounded health politicos around here are cuttin' in on my work. Scared of their jobs, I guess. Can't meet my competition. They ain't fair to me," Snell complained. "So the less ye talk, the better. After all, I'm helpin' ye get well and savin' ye money, so maybe ye can do *me* a favor and hold yer tongue."

Cherry muttered "Okay," although his lies made her very angry. One worthless man like this made many persons sick, and put the responsible house-to-house salesmen with their excellent wares in a bad light.

Snell went back to the shack to get the medicine. Cherry and Mrs. Grisbee watched him wrap three labeled jars in old newspapers. Snell appeared to be alone in the shack. A hunting rifle stood against the wall of his one room.

Cherry heard a whisper from one of the three men hiding in the back of the car. She could not make out the words.

The peddler came back to the car. He handed Cherry two jars, Mrs. Grisbee one jar.

"Here's yer Nature's Herb Cure, ladies, and I

guarantee satisfaction. That'll be fourteen dollars and fifty cents."

As instructed by the Food and Drug inspector, they opened their purses, paid Snell, and took the fake medicine. The sale was completed.

At that instant the car's back doors flew open and the three men sprang out. The sheriff grabbed and collared the surprised peddler.

"Sheriff, I ask you to arrest this man on this warrant," said the Food and Drug inspector, holding up a legal paper, "for delivering an adulterated, dangerous drug for introduction into interstate commerce."

"Who're ye? Let me go!" the peddler howled. "I ain't done nothing wrong!"

He lashed out and broke free and started to run. Dr. Hal came on the run from the other side. He seized Snell and hung onto him.

"Snell, this man is a Food and Drug inspector whom I've called in," Dr. Hal said. "Today's the last time you ever sell that foul medicine."

The peddler cursed and kicked at the young doctor.

The sheriff advanced with a pair of handcuffs. "All right, Snell, you might as well give in." He tried to put the handcuffs on him.

"It ain't fair!" the peddler yelled. "I been tricked!" He made a lunge toward Cherry at the open window of the car, but Hal quickly placed himself in the way. "I been framed! Why pick on *me*?"

"You'll get a fair trial," the sheriff said. This time he slid the handcuffs on Snell and snapped them shut.

"Here's yer Nature's Herb Cure, ladies."

Then, with the other handcuff on his own wrist, the sheriff pulled the peddler into the car. Mrs. Grisbee gasped, "Oh, me! Poor Snell!" The peddler heard and shouted accusations at her.

"Don't waste your pity on him," Cherry said to Phoebe Grisbee.

"Mr. Short! Dr. Miller!" the sheriff called. "What are you doing in the shack? Making an inspection?"

"Yes, looking for evidence," the Food and Drug inspector called back. "Just a minute—"

Cherry took off the dark glasses, carefully placed the two jars of the medicine on the car seat, then went to take a look inside the shack. It held a little crude furniture and a shelf full of merchandise, chiefly jars of the remedy.

"No sign that the concoction is brewed here," Dr. Hal said to her.

They left the shack untouched, padlocked the door, and returned to the car. The peddler snarled at Cherry, "So ye're the county nurse, Miss Hettie!" She did not answer him but got into the front seat with Hal and Mrs. Grisbee. Hal drove them back to Sauk.

On the way, the sheriff and the Food and Drug inspector tried to get Old Snell to talk. The sheriff had known Snell for years. "It won't hurt you, you know, if you'll tell us about the others."

"What others?" the peddler retorted. "Ye aim to find out anything, find it out by yourselfs."

They reached the Sauk jail in the county courthouse with their prisoner. Snell was turned over to a deputy sheriff, and locked up. The sheriff did not think they could take further action until tomorrow. He did not want to enter the abandoned farmhouse and risk a fight in the dark.

"Mr. Short, if you'd care to stay overnight at my house, you and I and Dr. Miller could talk over our strategy for tomorrow." The inspector agreed. "Ladies, thank you very much, both of you."

Mr. Short thanked them as well. Cherry handed over to him the three samples. Hal pressed her hand and whispered, "Good girl. You did a terrific job."

"Oh-h!" Mrs. Grisbee moaned. "Now that it's all over, I feel nervous as a flea."

Cherry said she would see her safely home. She did, returning on foot to her aunt's house.

Aunt Cora jumped out of her chair when Cherry came in.

"Cherry! Are you sick? You're so pale. What are you doing in those old clothes?"

Cherry giggled and collapsed into the nearest chair. "I'm perfectly healthy. Phoebe lent me her clothes to disguise myself."

The whole story came tumbling out. Cherry apologized to her aunt for not having been able to tell her sooner. She emphasized that it was still necessary to keep the situation a secret, since Floyd and the two St. Louis men still remained to be apprehended.

"Yes, by tomorrow Floyd will realize the peddler is missing—" Aunt Cora hesitated.

"That's it. Floyd may try to flee with all the evidence. The two St. Louis men may try to vanish, too. We'll have to move fast. And boldly."

CHAPTER XIII

Bad News

THEY HAD BEEN WAITING FOR TWENTY MINUTES now in the county health office—Hal pacing up and down, Cherry slumped down in a chair, both of them watching the clock's hands creep toward eight.

"He said yesterday he'd be here really early this morning," Cherry fretted. "He knows Floyd and those two men may run off at any minute."

Hal answered, "Maybe he's still with the sheriff, since he stayed at Mr. Steeley's house last night."

The telephone rang. Hal answered it on the first ring. He listened, said, "Oh, I see. . . . But the delay? . . . All right, sir. . . . We didn't know that."

He motioned to Cherry to come listen, too.

Mr. Short said: "I'm just leaving Sheriff Steeley's house to go talk to the newspaper editor." Sauk, the county seat, supported a weekly newspaper. "I have to talk with him about printing a warning to the public against the fake remedy. Persuading the editor often is the toughest part of this job."

It would require courage on the editor's part to attack a medicine which many people believed in. They would resent being told they were wrong, and the newspaper might or might not be able to convince them that the remedy was dangerous. Many were old friends of the peddler and would take Snell's side out of blind loyalty. In other FDA cases, editors had lost subscribers and had been sharply attacked. Mr. Short expected he would need a little time to explain the whole problem to the newspaperman. The Food and Drug inspector would rather go after Floyd first, but early this morning was the only time he could see the editor; he had tried in vain yesterday, and today the editor was leaving for the state capital to stay several days.

"The warning simply has to be published as soon as possible," Mr. Short said. "Too many people still have the medicine on hand from what you medical people tell me."

"Yes, they do," Hal said. "I see that a little delay is unavoidable."

"I expect to be at the editor's office for the next half hour or so," Mr. Short said.

"All right, sir," said Dr. Hal. "Where can we reach you after that?"

They decided Hal and Cherry should keep telephoning back to the county health office, to make contact through the clerk with Mr. Short.

Cherry sighed. Hal, hanging up, said to her, "No

use worrying about the delay. Mr. Short will meet us as soon as he can. Let's go about our day's work."

Starting out each in his own car, Cherry suggested to Hal that they stop first to see Jane. "I'd like to tell her that we nabbed the peddler, and find out anything we can about Floyd's moves."

"Good idea." Dr. Hal consulted his list of patients. "Luckily, I haven't any urgent cases today. Let's go."

They covered the ten miles to the Barker cottage in record time. On the way they passed the abandoned farm too fast for Cherry to have more than a glimpse. Reaching the Barker place, she noticed that Floyd's jalopy was not in the yard, but that did not prove he was not here on the premises.

They knocked, and when no one answered except the parrot, finally went in. The parrot was all excited. The bird hopped around in its cage and squawked:

"Never come back! Never come back!"

"What has that bird heard?" Hal said.

"Now, Mike," Cherry said soothingly to the parrot, but it flew at her against the bars of its cage.

"Won't tell where! Never come back!" it shrieked.

Something must have happened to send the bird into such a state. Where was Jane? Or Mrs. Barker? They heard sounds of weeping from the kitchen.

Cherry went in there, Hal following her. Mrs. Barker was seated at the kitchen table, crying as if her heart would break.

"Why, Mrs. Barker!" Cherry bent and put her arm around the old lady. "You mustn't cry like that."

"You'd cry too, if—if—your son—behaved—"

Dr. Hal took her hand and said, "Now control yourself, Mrs. Barker, and tell us how we can help you."

Emma Barker sniffled, wiped her eyes, put her glasses back on, and sat up straight.

"Floyd—my son . . . I never thought he'd just go off someday and leave me! Yes, sir, that's what he's done! This morning just before daylight I went into his room—I heard a lot of noise and banging around in there. There he was, packing his old suitcase in an awful hurry. When I asked him 'Where you going, Floyd?' he wouldn't tell me. Wouldn't tell me where or what for or—or for how long. He was putting everything he owns in the suitcase."

"Didn't he say anything?" Cherry asked. She felt terribly sorry for the old lady.

"All he said was—was— 'Kindly get out of my way, Ma, I'm in a hurry.' As if I couldn't see with my own eyes that he was running around like the devil was after him! And—and then when I kept pestering him with questions, he only said, 'I'm going a long ways away and I'm never coming back.'" Mrs. Barker broke into tears again. "Never coming back! Why? What's he got to run away for?"

Cherry and Hal stood beside Mrs. Barker in silence. They dared not tell her anything, not yet. Not with Floyd at large. Cherry wished fervently that they did not have to treat Emma Barker's son as if he were a public enemy. But apparently Floyd Barker was exactly that—and his running away pointed up his guilt. From the look on Hal's face he, too, was sorry to hurt Mrs. Barker, but he asked:

"What time did your son leave, Mrs. Barker?"

"He was up early and out of the house before sunup. Jumped into his car—didn't even stop to kiss me good-by until I ran after him—"

It was useless to ask where he had gone. Cherry could guess: he'd probably gone to the abandoned farm with its supply of ginseng plants. Those were too rare and valuable to leave behind. He needed them to continue his racket elsewhere. The reason he was in such a hurry to go away and never come back was all too obvious.

"Mrs. Barker," Dr. Hal persisted, "did anything happen, or did you or Floyd hear any news, that could have precipitated his going off?"

The old lady looked at him sharply. "That's a peculiar question. Nothing happened that I know of, except that Floyd went out for a long walk in the woods last evening and came home in an awful bad temper."

Cherry and Hal exchanged glances. Did this mean that Floyd had gone to the woods to see the peddler, and found the shack deserted and padlocked?

"What else happened last evening, Mrs. Barker?" Hal asked.

"Well, after Floyd came home from the woods, he hung around here for a few minutes. First he started to telephone somebody, then he changed his mind and hung up. *Then* he lit out again. I don't know for certain where he went, but I think he drove into town—"

"Into Sauk?" Hal asked.

"Yes. Because when he came back, a long time

later, he had a copy of the *Sauk Weekly Courier*
with him, and a bunch of cigars in his shirt pocket.
I especially noticed the cigars. Floyd never smokes
anything but that smelly old pipe of his. And I wish
to goodness he was here right now smoking it and
smelling up the house with it!"

"There, there," Cherry said softly. She was thinking about the cigars—the Sauk drugstore had the
only tobacco counter in town and sold cigars—and
the Sauk drugstore was a meeting place where you
could drop in to learn the local news. Surely someone in town must have seen the sheriff lead Old Snell
in handcuffs into the jail last evening. Someone must
have noticed the county medical officer, the county
nurse, Mrs. Grisbee, and another man, who was not
known to the local people, enter the jail. In a town
as small as Sauk, even the most insignificant event
drew comment. The peddler's arrest would be news
indeed. Floyd might have handed out cigars to persuade the men lounging around the drugstore to tell
him the details in full. Including, Cherry suspected,
anything they knew about a stranger who was the
Food and Drug inspector.

"Where's Jane?" Hal asked suddenly.

Mrs. Barker explained that Jane seemed upset
about their family crisis, and had tactfully "made
herself scarce." She was doing some mending out in
the yard. Hal seized upon seeing Jane as an excuse
to break away from the old lady. Cherry knew he,
too, was anxious to follow Floyd.

They found Jane seated in a canvas chair and sew-
ing. Her crutches lay on the grass.

"Floyd left!" Jane said when she saw Hal and Cherry. "Poor Mrs. Barker!"

"It'll be even more painful for her," Hal said, "if Floyd is caught and arrested. Assuming he's guilty. . . ." He told Jane rapidly how the peddler had been arrested yesterday, and how today's situation stood. "I think Cherry and I ought to go over to the old farm as fast as we can. Floyd might have gone there."

"From sunrise, when Floyd left here," Cherry figured aloud, "to now—that's three hours gone by."

"Well, let's go see if he's still there," Hal said. "It would take quite a while to pull up those ginseng beds."

"You mustn't enter the old farmhouse!" Jane exclaimed. "Suppose Floyd and those two men *are* in there—suppose they're armed. Three men to one—you're outnumbered, Hal."

"Hmm. We'd better phone the sheriff," Hal said. "He's armed; the Food and Drug inspector isn't, and hasn't power of arrest. Jane, to save time, would you . . . ?"

"*I'm* not going to call the sheriff to arrest my hostess's son," Jane said. She was greatly troubled. "I can't do that to her."

"Fair enough," Cherry said. "May I telephone from here to the Food and Drug inspector? Just to notify him that Floyd's gone off? And to ask him to join us at once at the old farmhouse?"

"We-ell." Jane looked unhappy. "Since your and Hal's safety is involved, I suppose you'd better."

"Hurry up," Hal said.

Cherry ran back to the house and, with Mrs. Barker's permission, used the telephone to call the Sauk newspaper office. Someone there said Mr. Short had just left with the editor to continue their discussion over breakfast. Cherry asked whether they had gone to Smith's Restaurant?

"No, they've gone to some friend's house," said her informant. "No, miss, I'm sorry, I don't know where you can reach him."

Cherry asked when or whether Mr. Short would return to the newspaper office, but her informant didn't know this either.

Another delay. More time for Floyd to get away! And for the two St. Louis men to get away. Cherry left word for Mr. Short at the newspaper office that she and Hal were going at once to the abandoned farm, and to join them there. "And tell Mr. Short," she said, "the situation is urgent." She called her own office and left the same message for Mr. Short with the clerk.

Then she called the sheriff's office, but Mr. Steeley and his deputy were out. What bad luck! Cherry left word, anyway, but this meant that she and Hal would enter the old farmhouse alone, without protection in case of trouble. She hoped that the highway patrolman might be in this area, or that the sheriff would telephone highway patrol headquarters.

Hal was already in his car, with the motor running. They'd leave Cherry's car here. Jane would explain it somehow to Mrs. Barker. Jane looked after them with an anxious expression as they tore off down the highway.

Even if Floyd and the men aren't in the house," Hal said, driving fast, "they may have left some evidence behind about where and how the remedy has been manufactured."

"Optimist!" Cherry scoffed at him. "You know they're too sharp to leave any traces."

CHAPTER XIV

~~~~~~

Through the Trap Door

SIX MINUTES LATER AT THE OLD FARM GROUNDS, they were stunned at what they saw. The big ginseng beds were bare! Someone had pulled up every last ginseng plant and root, leaving raw, freshly turned patches of earth.

"Not only to hide evidence," Hal muttered. "The racketeers must be taking the ginseng with them, so they can start up their racket in a new location," Hal guessed.

"To poison more people! Oh, Hal! Let's find them so Food and Drug can stop them."

They looked around for Floyd's jalopy or the "sportsmen's" car with the St. Louis license plates. They saw no cars here, not even any car tracks.

"Well, if they're in the house, they could have heard *our* car," Hal said. "We'll go in cautiously."

At the door they peered in and listened. The house was silent: Hal took a step or two down the

163

hallway and motioned Cherry to stay behind. She shook her head and followed him. A floor board creaked. They both halted as if frozen. Nothing happened, no one came. They started to move again.

The living room was empty as they passed it. Hal took a few long strides to look into the kitchen. His lips formed the word "Nothing." Cherry gained the doorway to the dining room, and nearly cried out in surprise. She drew Hal to look into the dining room. The long, tall, heavy, oak buffet, which stood against the wall adjoining the living room, was awry. Out of place, with one end dragged forward—someone had moved it! Why?

"Look at that!" Cherry whispered.

Hal did not understand what the buffet's being out of place meant. Cherry ran soundlessly across the dining room and felt along the wall behind the buffet. Under the old wallpaper she touched what might be a joining. She applied a little pressure, then more pressure, and a narrow section of the wall slowly swung in an arc on inside hinges. The opening was barely wide enough for one person to slip through. Cherry saw a narrow, oblong, windowless room.

"Cherry!" Hal whispered. "Don't go in there!"

"It's empty. Come on. But what a smell!"

The hidden chamber smelled overpoweringly of ginseng. A kerosene stove was in here. Was this where Floyd, or whoever, had brewed the remedy? Cherry looked around at the empty, stained shelves and the one old stool, with rings where pots and jars must have rested. Everything else was gone.

"Say"—Hal nudged her and whispered—"what's the reason for a concealed room in a farmhouse?"

"The Underground Railway—it had hiding places and escape routes," Cherry whispered back. "Look! Look down at the floor! A trap door!"

Cherry knelt and grasped its rusted iron ring. The trap door opened easily. Down below she saw only blackness.

Hal's hand came down on her shoulder. "Oh, no, you don't go down there!" Cherry furiously shook her head. "At least let me go first."

"Leave the trap door open," Cherry whispered, "so Paul Short and the sheriff can find us—if they come."

Hal eased his long length down through the opening in the floor. She heard a soft thud as he landed.

"It's black as pitch in here," he muttered. "Like a cave. Like the far end of the cave we found—"

"Must be a tunnel leading into the cave!"

Cherry crouched, then eased herself through the open trap door. Hal helped her down. Her foot slipped and landed on something softer than the earth floor. Cherry bent and picked up the thing and held it under the trap door where a dim light filtered through, from up in the dining room.

"Why, it's a book!" she whispered in surprise. "I can just make out the title page." It read: *The Compleat Housewife, 600 Receipts for Cooking and Remedies,* by E. Smith, London, 1753. "Hal, it's Mrs. Barker's old home-remedy book! Floyd took it—" She found a marker at the page with a formula for a ginseng remedy.

"Hang onto it." Hal took her hand. "Hold fast so we won't get separated in the dark." He started slowly ahead. After a minute's silence he said, "This is the other end of the tunnel, all right. But how'll we get past that pile of dirt and the blockade, into the cave and then into the open again?"

Suddenly they both grasped what must have happened down here. Someone had put up or retained the old barn door as a blockade, to prevent anyone in Riverside Park from entering the old farmhouse through the cave and tunnel. Floyd—or whoever had set up the blockade—evidently had dug earth out of the cave walls in order to accommodate the barn door. That would account for the pile of earth Hal had seen.

"Watch for daylight up ahead," Hal said softly to Cherry. "If we see daylight, we have a direct route for getting out of here. But if the passageway is still closed, we'll have to retreat back to the house. It won't be easy to scramble up through the trap door."

He meant that *if the three men were in the tunnel, they'd need to get away from them fast.* Cherry's heart pounded in alarm, but she said nothing and followed Hal. Presently she whispered:

"Listen! Do you hear something? A muffled sound—"

Hal paused. Cherry could not see him except as a blacker blur in the darkness. Then he said:

"Yes, I hear something. And I think I see a big patch of daylight. Scared? Want to turn back?"

"I'll go farther ahead if you will," Cherry whispered. "At least we could edge up closer and see what's going on. Though I'd rather not come face to face with—"

"Quiet!"

Hal and Cherry shrank back against the tunnel wall as someone—a man, judging by his heavy tread and breathing—ran past them on his subterranean way back to the farmhouse.

Farther down in the tunnel, at the open cave end, judging by the echo, a man's voice called roughly: "Where you going?"

The man near them shouted back, "I dropped the formula book somewhere in here! I got to find it!"

It was Floyd's voice. He struck a match, hunting on the earth floor, his back to them. Hal pulled Cherry away from the light of the matches. They stumbled into a shallow natural niche in the tunnel's earth wall and flattened themselves against it.

"Barker!" the same surly voice called. "You got that formula in your *head* by now! Come back here!" His voice echoed and re-echoed in the cave, and carried clearly up the tunnel.

"I *got* to find that book!" Floyd yelled back. He was far up the tunnel by now. "I'm just going back into the house for a minute—"

Cherry began to tremble. If Floyd went back into the house and noticed that the trap door was open, he'd be alerted to their presence.

"Barker!" This time Cherry and Hal saw the figure of one of the men silhouetted in front of the cave's opening. "We got to get away before those nosy kids bring the Food and Drug dick here! Do you want me to come and drag you back?"

"Okay, Benny, coming," Floyd called back. "I guess I can remember the formula all right."

In another minute he passed them again in the dark. Only then did Cherry let out a long breath in relief.

"Hurry up!" a second man's voice shouted. "I got the boats waiting, but we ain't finished loading. Give us a hand!"

Hal beside Cherry muttered, "So they're going to make their getaway down the river. With all the evidence! I want to see what direction they'll be going."

He moved nearer the cave, silent as a cat, half pulling Cherry after him. At one place Hal whispered:

"Look out—the old barn door and the pile of dirt should be about there. Don't stumble on them."

They picked their way, feeling for every step. But there was no pile of dirt. The passageway was clear.

They moved through the cave toward the glimmer of daylight. All was quiet at the far end of the cave—the three men must be busy loading the boats. Or already gone—? Hal and Cherry took advantage of these few quiet minutes to feel their way rapidly along the craggy cave walls. They came close to the cave's low, rocky opening.

Here, illuminated by daylight, they saw cardboard cartons full of jars of the fake remedy, burlap bags stuffed with ginseng plants and dried ginseng roots, and some ledgers. Here was the evidence!

"We can still turn back or get away," Hal said. "Or at least you can."

"No. I'm staying with you. If we can detain these men until Mr. Short gets here—"

Hal drew her back into shadow as the three men straggled into the cave. Floyd said, "Ezra will notice when we don't bring back two of his rented rowboats."

"He won't notice before five o'clock," the heavier of the two St. Louis men said scornfully. Cherry recognized the voice; he was Benny. "By then we'll be in the car and a long ways from here. Let him go find his boats adrift. Now hurry up with the loading."

The other man grunted. "Hurry! Hurry! I told you we should've beat it right after Barker saw the nurse prying around the house. But no, we had to stick around while Barker makes more of the stuff. We wait around to find out how well Snell can sell it in the towns. So now, it's hurry, hurry!"

"Shut up, Jake!" the heavy man growled. "Get a move on!"

The three men moved around the cave, picking up the heavy cartons and bags, stumbling a little on the cave's uneven floor. Hal and Cherry drew back as far as they could, trying to keep out of their way. Floyd, struggling with a load of medicine jars, stepped back a few paces, and brushed against them.

Floyd let out a howl. "Somebody's in here, Benny! In back of us—right here! I touched someone!"

Discovered, Hal sprang and gave Floyd a forceful shove toward Jake. "Cherry!" he yelled. "Run!"

Floyd stumbled into Jake. Jake staggered, dropping the bags of ginseng. He yanked a flashlight from his pocket and set its beam probing along the cave wall.

"Cherry, huh?" Benny repeated in the half-dark. "So it's the doctor and nurse!"

Hal aimed a kick at the spot of light shining in the darkness, but too late—the beam focused on Cherry, standing flattened and white-faced against the damp cave wall.

"Couldn't mind your own business," Benny rasped, reaching for his gun. Hal kicked again and this time the flashlight went flying. Still lighted, it bounced off the cave roof, then fell to the ground near Cherry. It struck a rock, and the light went out in a tinkling of shattered glass.

In the half-dark, Benny crouched with drawn gun —but the three indistinct figures blended together as Jake and Floyd descended on Hal from opposite sides, fists swinging. Hal sank quickly to the ground, and in the gloom the other two men traded hard blows before their gasps revealed them as allies. Cherry bolted for the cave opening.

Benny raced after her. Cherry stumbled, but regained her balance and kept running. A few more strides, and she was in daylight. "Help!" she yelled at the top of her lungs. She heard, away off in the distance, the high-pitched whine of a fast-moving car.

A moment later Benny had her by the arm. "Shut up!" he ordered. He dragged her roughly back toward the cave. "Save your breath. Nobody's around the park today except Ezra. He won't hear you—he's calking boats at the far end of the park. And nobody driving on the highway'll hear you, neither!" He thrust her into the cave.

Cherry saw Hal's lithe, rangy figure weave in and out between the two older, heavy men. One of them gasped in pain, as Hal's fist found his jaw. The second tallest figure, Floyd's, staggered back from the group. Jake swung, his flashy ring hitting Hal's forehead and cutting it open just above Hal's eye. Hal threw himself in a fury on Jake, aiming at the indistinct face before him with his clenched fists. Jake covered his face, then kicked viciously at Hal.

Hal dodged—and found Floyd's arm crooked around his throat from behind, pulling his head back. The grip tightened.

"Good!" Benny croaked. "Hold him. Jake, grab his knees."

Jake made a sudden lunge for Hal's knees and wrapped his arms around them. With Floyd and Jake holding him that way, Hal was helpless. Benny walked slowly toward Hal, pistol hanging loosely in his hand.

"You're not going to shoot him, are you?" Cherry gasped.

"No," Benny said agreeably, "just rough him up a little, that's all."

Cherry went cold, then desperately she searched with her foot on the dark floor of the cave. Her shoe touched the heavy metal flashlight.

She grabbed down for it, reached Benny's back at a run, and swung the flashlight crashing against the side of his head. He lurched crazily, then leveled his pistol at Cherry, shaking with anger.

A new voice rang out. "Drop your gun!" it commanded. "Put your hands up. Higher!"

Benny held fast to his gun. A shot rang out, loud as a blast of dynamite in the echoing cave.

Out of the shadows of the cave walked two highway patrolmen, each leveling a gun. Paul Short walked beside them. One patrolman was Tom Richards. A tendril of smoke floated from his gun.

Benny cursed and slowly lifted his arms. Jake and Floyd stood dejectedly with their hands raised. Ginseng plants and jars of medicine littered the cave floor.

"The sheriff's office relayed your telephone message to us," Richards said to Hal and Cherry. "We saw the open trap door. You shouldn't have come here by yourselves."

The highway patrolmen handcuffed Floyd to the two men. Richards prodded them at gun point out of the cave. At Inspector Short's request, the other patrolman collected the medicine jars, ginseng, ledgers, and old book as evidence. Mr. Short affixed a seal over the lid of one jar, signed and filled out the Food and Drug form on the seal.

Then he came over to Cherry and asked if she were all right. "Yes," she said, "and you certainly got here fast!"

Hal reported that the racketeers had two rowboats waiting at the riverbank, and a getaway car parked upriver. The highway patrolman turned to the Food and Drug inspector, and asked where he wanted to talk with the three men.

Mr. Short answered, "Well, the first thing we have to do is to give them a preliminary hearing before the United States commissioner at Des Moines.

He will decide whether they are to be held for a grand-jury investigation."

It was decided they would all drive to Des Moines that morning. Before undertaking the long drive, Hal and the three prisoners would receive medical care from Dr. Clark at his house.

"Hal," Cherry said, "you were terrific!"

Hal smiled at her. "You were fairly terrific yourself!"

CHAPTER XV

~~~~~~

The Whole Truth

CHERRY AND HAL SPENT A LONG AFTERNOON AS GOVernment witnesses at the preliminary hearing. They came home to Sauk to find Aunt Cora waiting for them.

"I heard!" Aunt Cora greeted them. "The whole town heard! But only bits and pieces— Are you both all right? Thank goodness! Here's some hot coffee. Now sit down, both of you, and tell me the whole story!"

"Yes, we've kept you in the dark too long," Cherry said. They all sat down together.

Hal gratefully accepted a cup of coffee. "Well, Mrs. Ames, the whole truth came out this afternoon in the office of a United States commissioner."

He explained that the commissioner, the Food and Drug inspector, a United States district attorney, and a court-appointed defense attorney had questioned Floyd Barker, Luke Snell, Benny Pike, and

174

Jake Dacey all afternoon to get the truth out of them.

"How did this fake drug racket start?" Aunt Cora asked them. "How did it operate?"

They told Aunt Cora that Floyd Barker had originated the scheme several months ago. It seemed that ever since Jane's great-uncle abandoned the old farm, Floyd had hankered to own it—a place where he could get away from his mother's lectures. He had hung around the deserted farm and had discovered the tunnel and the secret room. These had been blocked off for years.

Then one day Floyd discovered a big, wild patch of ginseng, a few miles from home. He recognized it, knew it was once used to make a home remedy, and looked it up in the ancient home-remedy book his mother had inherited. The book provided a simple ginseng formula for a "cure-all."

It occurred to Floyd to compound a ginseng medicine himself and sell it. Floyd secretly dug up the wild ginseng and transplanted the whole big patch to the deserted farm. It required little nurture and Floyd believed he had a bonanza.

Meanwhile, Floyd contacted two shady men who operated small rackets in and out of St. Louis. They were Benny Pike and Jake Dacey. Floyd had done several small unlawful jobs for them earlier when they drove through the county on dishonest business. Floyd glowingly described the scheme for making easy money to the two racketeers.

The two men were interested in his plan—provided the patent medicine would sell. Floyd told them he would prove it by selling it to local people. On this proviso, the racketeers advanced Floyd a little money needed to buy jars and ingredients, and to pay the peddler. The two men had misleading labels printed for Floyd in St. Louis; the printer was kept in ignorance.

Floyd shrewdly hired the door-to-door peddler in order to cover himself. He instructed Old Snell to sell the remedy as secretly as he could. Within a few weeks it caught on with the rural people. Almost at once it made money.

Floyd spent some of this money for more supplies. He gave a little to his mother, to keep her from asking questions. He kept some for himself and forwarded the rest to Benny and Jake.

Money made the St. Louis men grow still more interested. They promised Floyd, by telephone, that if the medicine continued to sell well for another month, their lawyer would figure out a way to market it more or less openly—and widely.

Floyd was well started on this project when Jane Fraser arrived to claim the abandoned farm. He had tried to persuade her not to come to Sauk, via his mother's letters in which Mrs. Barker innocently quoted Floyd about the old place being worthless. At least Floyd wanted time—a delay in September so he could harvest, dry, and compound last summer's ginseng crop and try out the remedy's wider sales. Jane's convalescence gave him time.

But Cherry upset his plans when she took Jane to see the farm. All the previous day and early that Saturday morning he had been drying ginseng roots in the hidden room, on a kerosene stove and wire trays. He was afraid that Cherry and Jane would notice the odor and heat, so he had tried to discourage the girls from going to the farm. Cherry did notice the heat and odor, and had expressed her curiosity to Jane, who in turn had mentioned it to Floyd and Mrs. Barker. After that, Floyd observed Cherry's movements closely.

When she pulled samples of ginseng at the deserted farm, Floyd figured she wanted them for identification. He watched her take them, then stole the roots back from Cherry's parked car, again hoping for a delay. But he overlooked one root on the car floor, and Cherry had had it analyzed.

Then Cherry visited the old farmhouse alone. She nearly caught him that day. He ducked into the hidden room just in time. At this point Floyd lost his nerve. He had the peddler go into hiding.

Floyd telephoned the two men in St. Louis. He thought they had better move the racket to some other location, away from the alert nurse and doctor. Floyd also sent good news about sales—in fact, he sent another sizable sum of money. The medicine was selling so well that Floyd thought it time to expand the racket, within some loophole of the law.

Benny and Jake came to see how Floyd made the medicine, and to discuss producing and marketing it on a wider scale, with advice from their lawyer, a shady character who knew how to get around the law. The two St. Louis men, bolder than Floyd, called the peddler out of hiding and sent him to sell the new drug in surrounding towns. They wanted to find out whether townspeople, as well as rural people, would buy the new remedy. Some did buy it. Next, the swindlers planned to stock the cure with druggists, if possible.

Floyd warned the two St. Louis men that Cherry was alert to the source of the remedy, the ginseng at the abandoned farm. But they figured: what if medical people find it worthless? Though many patent medicines are helpful, plenty of worthless ones sell. They figured that Floyd's racket could operate just within the law.

The swindlers were wrong. They underestimated the Food and Drug Administration.

"I heard," Aunt Cora said, "that you two cornered those men today. How'd you find them?" Cherry explained how the buffet, jutting way out into the dining room, had given them away. "Hmm," said Aunt Cora. "You'd think they would have been more careful."

Hal said the men had admitted being careless, because they had been in a terrific hurry this morning. During the night, all they had been able to do in the dark, using a dim light, was to move things from the concealed room down into the tunnel, and Benny and Jake took down the old barn door in the tunnel and shoveled the dirt out of the way. Once daylight came, Floyd had pulled all the ginseng up, while Benny and Jake went for two rowboats, hid them at the riverbank near the cave, and then left the car at another hidden location for the getaway.

"What about that pile of dirt and the old barn door?" Aunt Cora asked. "Did Floyd blockade the tunnel?" Cherry answered her:

"Floyd said he found the tunnel that way when he was a boy. Apparently whoever lived there long ago closed off the tunnel so nobody'd wander into the cave and come walking into his farmhouse. Whoever it was, dug the dirt out of the tunnel walls to make room to wedge the barn door in there."

"Well," Hal said, getting to his feet, "those men committed a federal offense, and can get three years in prison. They're in prison now, awaiting trial. I guess you heard that, Mrs. Ames."

She nodded. "I also heard that the Food and Drug Administration will seize any of the remedy that's still available, and warn the public against it."

Cherry stood up, too. "Aunt Cora, if you'll excuse us, Hal and I want to stop in to see Mrs. Barker."

Cherry and Hal did not know whether or not Mrs. Barker had heard of her son's arrest. Had anyone been heartless enough to tell her? If not, Cherry and Hal wanted to break the news as gently as possible.

She knew. Jane had laid out supper on the kitchen table, but neither she nor Mrs. Barker was able to eat.

"A neighbor called me up and told me," Emma Barker greeted Hal and Cherry. "It's all right, children, you don't have to wear such long faces."

"We're sorrier than we can tell you," Cherry said.

"If it were anyone but *your* son—" Hal muttered. "Sorry, terribly sorry."

"You have to do your duty, I know that." Mrs. Barker's eyes were red from weeping, but she was self-controlled. "Floyd deserves to be punished. He injured a lot of people with that Nature's Herb Cure. I just want to know one thing. How long will my son be—be away?"

Jane and Cherry exchanged glances. Hal had a hard time telling her it probably would be three years. Was there anything they could do for her, Cherry and Hal asked, anything at all? Mrs. Barker shook her head.

Jane said warmly, "I want Mrs. Barker to come and live with Mother and Bill and me. We'll turn that old house into a happy place, you'll see. Now we can go ahead and repair the place—thanks to you two."

Hal was embarrassed and Cherry said no thanks were necessary. All they wanted was to see that ankle completely healed. That would be very soon now.

Jane said cheerfully, "Did I tell you that I've got a job? Just this afternoon! The owner came by to talk over the letter of application I'd sent in. It's a good and interesting job at the big motel restaurant near Muir. That's thanks to you two, as well." She did not want to rejoice in view of Mrs. Barker's trouble, but Jane's relief and happiness showed in her face. "I'm going to telephone Mother and Bill the good news tonight."

"Well, don't tell your mother I'm coming to live with you," Mrs. Barker said. "I can manage in my own house, thank you! I'll be over to visit every day, though, I expect."

"Maybe you'll change your mind when you meet Bill," Jane said. "That reminds me! We'll be married in Sauk. Of course you're invited to the wedding. Cherry, I want you to be maid of honor."

Cherry accepted with great pleasure. She felt sure she could persuade Aunt Cora to let her give Jane a wedding breakfast or reception.

Hal cleared his throat and said he'd been reading up on new therapy which might be just the measures for Bill.

"You see," Mrs. Barker said bravely, "things *do* work out for the best." Hal and Cherry both kissed Mrs. Barker good-by. They said "Cheers!" to Jane.

In the car, driving home to Sauk in the darkness of evening, Cherry thought of the patients she had missed seeing today—well, she'd catch up later this week—and about the 4-H Club youngsters— about the monthly report to be sent to her supervisor, Miss Hudson—and about going to the monthly district meeting with other rural nurses. . . .

"Wake up, Cherry!" Hal said, pulling up in front of Aunt Cora's house. "You're home."

"I wasn't asleep, just daydreaming. There's so much important health work to be done in the county—"

"You'll do it," Hal said. "We'll do it together."

That was a happy prospect. Cherry said good night to Dr. Hal, and went into the house to her long-suffering aunt.

"Praise be it's all over!" said Aunt Cora. "I never in all my born days— I dread to think what you'll be up to next, Cherry."

"Wait and see," said Cherry, smiling.